13 POETS FROM LONG ISLAND

Bushwickborn Productions, Inc. / Pope Brothers Ink

2023

Made in the USA
Monee, IL
09 September 2023

6c65ddcd-7e02-4ab5-bb31-983888173f9aR01

13 POETS FROM LONG ISLAND

Writing Poetry, Anthology Volume 4
2023
Works from the class of former Nassau County
Poet Laureate Evelyn Kandel

2023

Bushwickborn Productions, Inc. / Pope Brothers Ink
Elmhurst, New York 11373

Edited by John A. Valenti 3rd and Evelyn Kandel
Copyright © 2023 by John A. Valenti 3rd, Evelyn Kandel

Bushwickborn Productions, Inc. / Pope Brothers Ink
at
13PoetsfromLongIsland@gmail.com

Library of Congress Cataloguing-in-Publication Data
HARDCOVER ISBN: 979-8-9889193-2-2
PAPERBACK ISBN: 979-8-9889193-0-8
E-BOOK ISBN: 979-8-9889193-1-5

Book Design by John A. Valenti 3rd

Front Cover Art: Long Island Sound at Horton Point, Southold
Rear Cover Art: Orient Point Ferry, Orient
Photos by John A. Valenti 3rd

EVELYN KANDEL
HATTIE ABBEY • HANK BJORKLUND • VICTORIA BJORKLUND
LILA EDELKIND • JOHN LANGE • GEORGE PAFITIS • GLADYS THOMPSON ROTH
SHEILA SAFERSTEIN • GEORGE STRAUSMAN • JOHN A. VALENTI 3RD
SUSAN ASTER WALLMAN • JUDITH ZILBERSTEIN

This book is dedicated to Gladys Thompson Roth,
who turned 100 years young in June 2023,
and to the memory of two beloved class members
— Jack B. Weinstein and Aaron Reisfeld

Prologue

Appendix

PROLOGUE

A Note from Our Poet Laureate

This is my fourth time writing an introduction to a book of poems by my students in the Writing Poetry class. Class began in Great Neck's Adult Education program in 2009 and we've been meeting for three sessions a year for fourteen years. We made changes recently, especially when the pandemic hit; it was necessary for us to hold classes on Zoom and to say farewell to the school. It also became a private enterprise. Our early attempts at virtual meetings were more like a comedy show than a serious educational endeavor. But, we persevered and one of our newest students, Victoria Bjorklund, who joined in 2021 with her husband Hank, turned confusion into comfort when she took over the reins of Zoom technology.

A sigh of relief — and gratitude to her for relieving me.

There have been students who came for a while then moved on. But, here are those who came and stayed: Judith Zilberstein, who holds the record at 42 sessions, joined in Fall 2009, followed by researcher and revisionist George Pafitis, who joined in Spring 2010.

In 2012, I was honored to have the multi-talented Gladys Thompson Roth and Hattie Abbey, my party-girl partner, join — and, two years later, George Strausman brought his wonderful sense of humor. With a matching sense of humor, Susan Aster Wallman, retired from a creative position in a literary organization, joined our group in 2015.

The year 2017 brought Jack Lange, a man of wit and wisdom, professor of philosophy, and a brilliant educator; talented singer Sheila Saferstein also joined. Three super newcomers turned 2021 into a bonanza: Lila Edelkind, not only an excellent poet, but an artist and craftswoman; and, Hank and Victoria Bjorklund, a very special couple. Both Bjorklunds joined with little poetic experience, but became very good poets almost immediately. Victoria is a prominent lawyer, very involved as a board member in non-profit causes, while Hank, also a lawyer, was a professional football player for the New York Jets. Yet, he writes with such original language and emotion it sounds as if he has written poetry his whole life. And finally, 2022 brought John A. Valenti 3rd, a journalist for *Newsday,* who learned of the class when he interviewed me about my Poet Laureateship for Nassau County and my military experience in the U.S. Marines. John had been writing poetry, so he was comfortable when he joined in Fall 2022, then re-joined for Winter and Spring 2023. As an experienced writer he said he was impressed by the poetry being written — and I think he will be a "stayer" with our group.

Evelyn Kandel

THE POETS

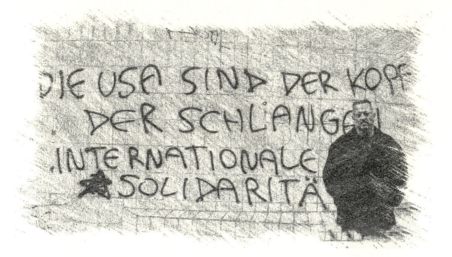

John A. Valenti 3rd

John Valenti is a nine-time Pulitzer Prize-nominated and national award-winning journalist who has worked for *Newsday* since 1981 and appeared on hundreds of radio and TV shows, including *NPR* and *Good Morning America.* He headed the 1997 *Newsday* investigation into New York Islanders owner John Spano, resulting in a federal fraud conviction, earning First Place in the Associated Press Sports Editors national competition for Best Investigative Reporting and inspiring the Emmy Award-winning *ESPN* 30-for-30 episode *Big Shot.* Author of the critically acclaimed *Swee'pea* (Simon & Schuster / Atria Books) about New York City playground basketball star Lloyd (Swee'pea) Daniels, Valenti was part of a two-man team whose investigation of the University of Nevada-Las Vegas led to the resignation of coach Jerry Tarkanian — and a death-penalty ban from the NCAA Tournament. Honored multiple times by The Society of the Silurians, Valenti once posed as a limo driver to get a story, was threatened by a mob associate out of *Wise Guy* and has interviewed a wide array of subjects, including Michael Jordan, Mike Tyson, Mario Andretti, Wayne Gretzky, Steffi Graf, Pele and the first two men to walk on the Moon, Neil Armstrong and Buzz Aldrin. A traveler, he's been to 45 states and more than 20 countries. A candidate for the NASA Journalist in Space Project and graduate of Oceanside (N.Y.) High School and Hofstra University, he has been writing poetry most of his life.

It's Us, Not Them

The latest one began like this:
with meteoric rhetoric about former satellite nations,
about how they'd done the unconscionable,
turned their backs on the Mother who'd loved them;
the rest of the free world, awash in bravado,
saying don't dare punish those you call your children
or we'll soon anger, shame you with contempt

In the blink of an eye it'd become
the slaughter of innocents, the slaughter of innocence
One more statesman having guaranteed peace;
one more bad man beating on a drum

And the victims put on a brave face,
pledging they'd forever stand strong, persevere,
ever-steadfast in their conviction,
as cities fell to ruin, laid waste; missiles and bombs,
the barrage of bullets and of artillery shells,
the rumble of armor and the mumble of soldiers,
dancing in time to the bombast of a madman
— a madman gone madder still

And the world stood idle by, all talk;
its ideological argument for reason,
its plea for humanity, for civility, for end, disregarded
as wave after wave after wave unfurled

And for the countless it continued, onrush, as it always does,
as it always has: in despair, in ruin, in death;
body counts for the victors, blood loss for the losers,
the shaking of heads, of those barking from the sidelines, dogs,
saying too bad no one listened, saying too bad, what a shame,
not any of the one understanding history always repeats itself
That we're its enablers and its moralizers, on and on, *ad infinitum*
For we are hunters disguised as gatherers,
are warmongers disguised as peacemakers and as diplomats
For we are bystanders and admirers when we need be apostates
For we claim to be knowing of the future,
while we remain oh so illiterate of the past
For we are flawed. For we are mankind

Penn Station, 1985

Final destination
Bag ladies load lifetimes
into old Macy's shopping bags
as teenaged boys, gleam gone from their eyes,
wink at me in hopes I'm the chicken man
I'm not
TA cops and New York's Finest
stand around making time
with young girls in the terminal
What's your number, honey?
I'm just sixteen
Fine by me, I'll never tell
Punks of a Brave New World
amble by;
FTW 69,
that's what it says
Crew-cut girl stops to talk to Mother Vagabond
Does she really think Pathmark's No. 1?
Young bitch drawing on a cigarette
uses the 30-second pay phone
for the quickest of calls
In green fatigues, red sweat socks and Army boots,
her T-shirt reads *Penguins from the Frozen Waste*
At least she sounds intelligent
You won't get laid, anyhow
Trench-coat man with purple ski cap
rumbles by
one leg shorter than the other
He smiles at phone girl as she
snickers, turns the other cheek
and walks away
munching ice cold pizza
Anything tastes good this late at night
Trench-coat thinks: Even her

Track 20
Will my train ever come?
I don't think so
and I have to take a piss
— monster piss

Chicken boy circles slow
He's got a likely customer:
"Water of love," I hear him say
Get me out of here
Forsake my body, my soul,
my piss,
from the place where drunkards crash
with lightning regularity
(It does strike twice here — and more)
"Hey, you got a buck," I hear someone say
Get the *fuck* away from me
The cleaning boys clean
with final futility
in the underground home
of permanent dirt
And I watch and wonder,
in anger and curiosity
I've lost my virginity
here in Penn Station, NYC,
with the losers as we wait for dawn

A Bottle Thrown

Stranger in some distant land,
just a note to understand
that I am lost until I'm found;
still, my hopes and dreams abound
You'll know not where
the land I'm from
If you've not seen,
if you'll not come
to rescue me, to free my soul,
wearied from the depths of woe
A written note, from deep morass;
a bottle thrown, note inside glass,
into an ocean, on waves to crest,
until afar it comes to rest
I trust and hope you understand
that I am but, I am a man,
lost amid some restless sea
— awaiting answers, seeking me

5

Grandma's Kitchen, Mine

I stand at the stove, cooking
And in this moment I am struck by a thought
unexpected, yet clear; one I've had
many times in moments like this

I wonder what my grandmother would think
if she could see me now
If I could share one more meal, this meal,
with her . . . after all these years
Gone a lifetime now, she's been,
decades removed from painstaking death;
still a dagger, Lou Gehrig, damned Yankee
I fight hard not to think of her
as she wasted away, life choked out; ALS
Rather me and her on a Sunday morning
on line at the Bohack's; those shopping carts
Her, trading stories with the cashier
Or back on old Myrtle Avenue, under the El
Or maybe rummaging through stores on Love Lane
Or stopping at farm stands
along the old North Road
Buying duck eggs, sorting Brussels sprouts;
sprouts like the ones I'm doctoring now
Different, far different, from those she made
My take on all I've learned,
since she's been gone

I can still taste the cold coffee ice cream
and warm mocha cake
Can still feel her smile as she says:
"I made this, Johnnie, just for you"
I wonder what she'd say now if she could
share this meal, one meal,
seeing what I've made, am making;
seeing what I've done, what I've become
All of it, since she's been gone
A career, a lifetime, a life; mine
I wonder what it'd all be like if you could ever
just wish for a moment, then get it
What it'd be, what you'd ask

6

For me, I don't wonder this one bit now
I know it, it's clear. Clear through my tears
As it always is, has been, when this moment hits
Hits me like a Mack truck or a freight train;
like a tidal wave, cascading; crushing

It'd be one meal, just one
One meal, cooked for my grandmother
if just so I could tell her:
"I made this, Grandma, just for you . . . "

Some Men

Some men die too soon
Some men, not soon enough

Get the Picture

I drew pictures of planes as a kid
Warplanes
And I wondered what it must be like
to have someone send you into battle
You, just a kid
Telling you it'd be alright to kill,
alright to be killed,
in defense of a principle,
in defense of someone else
And if we're alright with that
— or if we just need to be
Because evil must be stopped;
stopped, hang the expense
And I wonder if the rest of us
appreciate the cost of the sacrifice
when we complain about
our dinner being cold
and fail to be
thankful
it wasn't us

My Old Man

I can still see my old man
as he walks across the parking lot
towards the creek, bucket in hand;
his look, of resignation

It's November and a stiff wind blows,
the first chill of coming winter
insinuating itself on our world
He is middle age; me, barely a teen
I watch as the men, all business,
stare down on us from the platform

They're waiting for the morning train
and they're giving us the once-over
I glare at them, hard; me, just a kid
And my old man, he never looks up
Just walks, across worn pavement
Just walks, numb to the elements
Walks, intent, on what it is must be done
One broken step at a time

There's no water in our apartment
No heat, no water, and we are going out back
to the creek, buckets in hand, to fetch us some
To fetch some water, so we can do our business
To fetch us some, so we can save one last
small bit of dignity in our lives
Above us, those men turn
to one another,
amused

We are not beggars, we are not criminals
But those men do not know us,
do not know our circumstance
Do not know what we are,
do not care

We are father and son
We are not anything these days
but poor

We are walking across littered asphalt
for buckets of creek water
to flush our toilet
And in this moment I understand
I am just a boy
and still do not know much of the world

What I do know is we are of little consequence
To those men, not the least
I know this is a thought that will last me forever
That men will judge, no matter

Metal Fatigue

They wheeled me in on the gurney,
explained one last time
what it was they were going to do
They'd slice me open, cut me apart,
saw through bone, make me bionic
One hip, one morning; the other, two days hence
My body as I knew it to be gone forever
From imperfectly fine to near-catastrophic
in a mere matter of months; go figure
No explanation. Idiopathic, the doctor'd said
Idiopathic, yes. As in we really have no clue
And now, here I was, stretched out, waiting
Waiting for the anesthesia
Waiting for the knockout punch
One last moment, before it forever changed
Changed for the better, changed for the worse
Because, it all came with hope
Because, there was no going back
How do you get to a place?
It was something I'd always wondered
Sometimes, you plan to get somewhere
Sometimes, there's no rhyme or reason at all
They say shit happens. Oh, don't I know it
My friends joke, all this gadgetry,
I've become the *Six-Million-Dollar Man*
I tell them I'd much rather have it
in my pocket than in my body
And still, I say, it beats most of the alternatives
Not all, but most

On the Platform

On the platform I stand
Early morning, New York City
Watching it all go by, waiting on a train
And I see the faces of the world
Of places distant, of lives forever unseen
And I think of how I'd always hoped
to one day hit the lottery
To have more, to have opportunities;
have things I don't now have, haven't had
And I look harder, watch longer
and I see the places where
dreams never take root, are snuffed
Where they die little deaths each day,
hard to the realities of barren, scorched earth
and ruthless, unflinching circumstance
of losing bets, of un-winnable hands
And I realize, in this moment,
I've had my ticket, within grasp, all along

I'm Tired

I'm tired
Tired of working my life away
Tired of not having enough of what I want or need
Tired of nonsense and of broken promises
Tired of customer service reps claiming they're here to help
Tired of the fact their service is all lip, nothing more
I'm tired of politics and politicians
— and not just the ones you don't like
I'm tired of them all
I'm tired of fighting battles I can't win
I'm tired of fighting them, anyway
I'm tired of incompetence, of people who don't care enough
Tired of ignorance and unwillingness to learn
Tired of the disregard for hard-fought freedom
Tired of the lack of consideration
Tired of the fact there's never enough time
Tired of the lack of simple human kindness
I'm tired

Change Come Slow

Change comes like a lightning bolt
Or a heart attack, or a hurricane, or tropical rain
An accident, out of the blue
A message without meaning
A note to me and you
Sometimes, it's a lot of nothing
Others, more than we know
Change comes fast
Change come slow

The Train Car

The old cattle car stands on the siding still
Abandoned, weathered, worn to the elements
A victim of time, for now here to remind
Trees to embrace it, a world, green and ever-last
The grass, new-mown, new-sown,
amid the rust, the rot; amid the dew
The nearby chamber seems so antiseptic,
cold and concrete — once thought a shelter, a haven,
a shower for life; now known to be anything but
And I shiver at the moment, at the horror, at the end
Men, women and children; sisters, brothers, aunts and uncles,
parents, grandparents, families — all those who came before
under far different circumstance
Under the iron fist of invitation
The unwelcome, unwanted, unseen; *the un-being*
And how their neighbors turned that blind eye:
to the buildings, to the terror, to the stench;
to the inhumanities, to the indignities
Going about their business, going about their living,
as swords fell and trains rumbled on by,
day and night, night and day,
for weeks, months, and for years, without end;
to a place everyone knew, but pretended not
That old cattle car, now alone, there still;
its fading woodwork the color of dead blood and live forest moss
Worn to the elements, its fade yet forever indelible
to anyone with a conscience, with a heart
With a shred of humanity, willing to listen,
willing to learn, willing to see

HANK BJORKLUND

Hank Bjorklund played football for Princeton University and the New York Jets and began writing poetry as a way of coping with a chronic brain condition possibly caused by repetitive head hits he experienced in tackle football, from Pop Warner to the NFL. After retiring from football, Bjorklund graduated from Hofstra University Law, becoming a business attorney in New York City. After years of practice, he earned an MS degree and became an educator and coach. He also appeared in numerous television commercials and print ads and completed the acting program at the New Actors Workshop in NYC. After hospitalization in 2016 due to his brain condition, he experienced dysautonomia — i.e., severe disruption of his autonomic nervous system. Thanks to intensive physical and neuropsychological therapy, his systems now appear to be stabilizing. An inductee into the Nassau County High School Athletic Hall of Fame, an All-Long Island football player and runner-up for the Thorp Award as the best football player in Nassau at North Shore High, Bjorklund is the author of *Head Hits I Remember: My Brain, Dysautonomia and Football* (2023).

Hiking in Spain

I lay down
in a mountain swale
No wind or sound
could touch me
Noise of nothing
echoed in my head
— enormous silence
Almost unbearable,
solitude enveloped me,
melding me
to the mountain
A noticed miracle
I would never forget
— and would hurt
to remember
I wanted to stay,
but had lingered long
The others had passed,
so I moved on

Dear Fear

This is what you call a "Dear John Letter"
Yes, I am breaking up with you,
throwing you out on the street,
changing all locks, bolting all windows and doors
In other words, I am severing all ties,
cutting all connections!
I want you out of my life

Oh, I know what you're thinking
You're thinking you'll work your way back
into the house of my head,
just like you've done in the past
But you should know I've found somebody new,
somebody who'll stand by me
Her name is courage
— and we'll be waiting

Only Scars

You have no open wound
Just scars of thickened skin,
reminding you who you are,
showing you where you've been

Scars throb from time to time,
can pulse with piercing pain
Acceptance eases suffering
and you carry on again

Life and love always cut
a gash against the grain
Leave you with an open wound
that always bleeds the same

Let scars build thick and hard,
'til every scab is pruned;
'til you know with honest heart,
you have no open wound

Ode to Blues

I love you
in all your forms
I always have

I love you
on a cloudless day,
when you fill skies

I love you
when your azure
flickers off waters
of Azalea Pool

I love you
when you're dark,
like the lapis crayon
or night skies

14

I love you
when I lose myself
in your rhythm
and feel your soul

I even love you
when you possess me
and I melt, melancholy,
under your soft spell

Rock me now
in a cradle
of all your colors
I love blues

Fire of Life

Before I was born I walked alone
across an endless field of green-gold
under an open magenta sky
No past to break me,
no future to rob now

I felt you in the distance,
your heat inexorably drawing me
into the fired belly of life

Now, youth has flown from our faces
But a photograph shows
your skin, porcelain pure;
your hair, dark as night between stars;
your smile, still deep as light and love

Our days are beautifully ordinary,
strung together like perfect pearls
tightly tied on a silver strand

May this be forever
here, with our three furry felines
— our coats side by side,
hanging in the hallway

Gunmakers Rule

NRA screams to say:
Get your guns without delay!
If blue donkeys have their way
they'll take your precious guns away
Sixty dead at the Mandalay Bay?
Bill O'Reilly heard to say:
"Freedom's" price we have to pay
Say what? Say what?

Gunmakers rule,
their shareholders drool
Red elephants their tool
All guns are cool
Guns in every room and closet
You only need a small deposit
Automatic, so dramatic
Rapid fire, your desire
Not old enough to buy a car?
Buy a gun, that's no bar
Gunmakers rule

Bullets flyin', kids are dyin'
Still they're deaf to mothers cryin'
Spinnin' nonsense some are buyin'
Children's dreamin' turns to screamin'
Safe in school has lost all meanin'
Hard believin' what we're seein'
Gunmakers rule

Playin' on a city street?
A gunshot sound — and you're dead meat
Drivin' in the family car?
Road rage roars, you don't get far
Standin' in a public place?
Bullets race across your face
The whole damn thing a huge disgrace;
a pox upon the human race
Gunmakers rule

Power and money trump human lives
So they'll keep tellin' damnable lies

More guns the answer, the biggest lie
More guns we know more people die
Guns don't kill people they're always sayin'
It's people who raise the price we're payin'
It's people with guns who do the killin'
Red elephants sit, more than willin'
to let it slide — despite the spillin'
Gunmakers rule

Read the Second Amendment of the Constitution
If you're smart and honest you'll see the solution
It's state militia have the right to carry
Not every crazy Tom, Dick and Harry
That was the overwhelmin' opinion
— 'til the NRA seized dominion
Identity Politics, sad to say
My God, what a terrible price we pay

When Gunmakers rule

A Memory Washed Clean

We crawled up the long driveway;
me, flapping my legs against the back seat,
spouting every bad word I knew
Such glee, such glee
You, driving and scolding me as a naughty boy,
threatening to wash my mouth out with soap
I laughed and said: "Poo poo, pee pee, ha ha ha"

We entered the house
You marched me to the kitchen,
set out a bar of soap and a glass of water,
then ordered me to take a bite and chew
Laughing, I did as I was told
Wow! I spit and spit to get the soap out
and gargled with water 'til my mouth sparkled

I learned a valuable lesson that day:
Using naughty language in front of Gram
was in *really* bad taste

My Dearest Self

Your life is a roller coaster:
arduous ascents, stomach-churning descents,
centrifugal turns that threaten to derail
and send you plummeting to hard cement
Yet, there are stretches where the track
is flat and you dream of a silk-smooth ride
Your life is a warm blanket cuddling you in love,
soft as velvet and babies' fleece
There is peace and permanence under its covers,
and your hands clutch and grasp its edges
to keep the miracle alive
— her breath, her voice, her touch here, now
But nothing is forever and the harder you hold
the more it feels like sand slipping through your fingers
Your life is a long watch on the mirador
seeking God's face, listening for His voice,
waiting for those moments when you hear
nature's cries, see signals from the skies
that tell you something in you never dies

No Place Like Here

You dreamed you grabbed a comet's tail,
shook it hard to feel the rattle
Rode it to the edge of time,
where galaxies did battle
No longer were you laden
with heavy pull of Earth
You soared among the stars to see
heavens' giving birth
You dreamed you surfed a tidal wave
on shoulders of a whale,
and briny's deepest canyons
were well within your pale
You breathed beneath the waters,
fleet-finned as any fish,
and Poseidon, King of Oceans,
would grant you any wish
Then morning sun pierced your eyes,
brought you back to ground

Heard her breathing next to you,
smiled softly at the sound
There's nowhere else you'd rather be
than right here in your world
Another day, another way,
life's miracles unfurled

He Swears This to Be True

My friend told me this story and swears it to be true:
A man had lost his wife of 60 years and felt an emptiness
that had no bottom, a grief more constant
and intense than any physical pain
He was lost beyond finding and had no will to hope
He and his wife had loved to walk the beaches
on the South Shore of Long Island
She loved to wander among the flotsam and jetsam,
searching for shells and sea glass
Her dream was to find a bottle with a message inside,
a message that reached beyond time, she would say
On every walk, she brought a bottle containing her message
of love and hope. He would cast it into the sea,
throwing it beyond the breakers
She always wrote the same message:
"Love, there is hope in tomorrow"
And she would always write her initials at the bottom,
as if somehow, the finder would know who the sender was
He had not walked the beach since her death three years ago
But there he was, walking. Bereft, he harbored the notion
that he would enter the water and swim to beyond the horizon
 Alone on the shore, he stopped to face the sea
He felt something beneath his foot
It was a bottle, like the empty cinnamon bottles
she would use to carry her messages
His hand trembled as he reached down to grasp it,
fumbled as he struggled to unscrew the top
Inside was her message and her initials
But there was something else;
something he had never seen before
She also had written: "I am with you"
He fell to his knees and wept tears
that came from the depths of his being
He would never take that swim to beyond the horizon

Tender in the Night

My father
lay down beside me,
held my hand
in silence;
a sweet, still, caring kindness
'til sleep held my hand

Gazing Out the Window

I was gazing out the window at the naked trees
in my neighbor's yard; not a leaf left on a twig
I stared at the severed limb that snapped years ago

My mind moves where it will
— and settled on my father and that day he said:
Now you know where you got your athletic ability
Years had passed since my parents told me I was adopted,
but my biological "family" had recently made contact
There was anguish in my father's words; for him and for me

Yes, I said. I know where it comes from,
how it was revealed and how it blossomed
Who spent endless hours playing catch with me
in the yard and in the street?
Who taught me to throw a curve, to throw like a catcher
with a rifle arm; to throw a football with a perfect spiral?
Who taught me to hit a baseball with power
and to bunt with a delicate touch?
Who taught me to punt a football;
to make it spin and boom, far and high?
Who taught me to hike the ball
that first year when I played center?
Who helped coach my Pop Warner Football
and Little League Baseball teams?
Who let me play in the Majors with the 12-year-olds
when I was 10, because that's where I belonged?
Who waited at the courts while I shot endless baskets?
Who built the high-jump bar in the backyard
to help me break the school record?
Who taught me to explode out of the sprinter's block?

Who came to every game I ever played, in any sport,
from the age of nine to the NFL?
Who never gave me false praise, but always encouraged me
and never, ever criticized me if I made a mistake
— or didn't play well?
Who did that Dad?
It wasn't the guy who spent himself on a moment's pleasure
It was you. It was you, Dad. It was *always* you

My eyes never left the snapped limb
as gratitude welled within me
And I thought how strange it was
that the tree should be left so naked
in the dead of winter

Still Rising in Me

My hand on his chest
It rises still, then silent
Now, rising in me

Whispering Wind

I am what I am
I live in a cottage perched on a wall of stone clouds
I used to wander miles of sea that roiled outside my window
I love to remember days spent
in canyons of Poseidon's briny kingdom
I am a word dancer because
I answer cries of gulls who dance with roar and whisper of wind
I have a hand with a beating heart that finds my mind and pen
meandering like lost travelers in the night
I had an idea for a poem,
but I gave it to the osprey as mud to build her nest
I worry about our turning world and its whirling words
that make us dust
I am a poet because I am a man with no choice in the matter
I am accomplished at inviting words I know and words
I wish I knew to dance with me to music of the gloaming
I created a moon beam from a feather of an angel's wing
I live in blood and bone, and by the grace of a higher power
I am what I am and so much more than what I know

George Strausman

Born in 1924, George Strausman grew up in Belle Harbor on the Rockaway Peninsula in Queens, New York. A graduate of Far Rockaway High School, Strausman attended the City College of New York, worked as a ship builder and in aircraft engineering, becoming a resident of Great Neck, New York, in 1946. Vice president of Strausman Construction, his company built single-family housing on Long Island in Hempstead, East Meadow, Westbury and Levittown, as well as apartment houses in Great Neck and the Mayfair nursing home in Hempstead. He also was a custom builder of homes in Great Neck and East Hampton, and headed construction projects in New Jersey and Virginia. Strausman also was operator of Grace Plaza Nursing Home from 1972-2003. Proud husband of Nancy, father of three, grandfather of 11 and great-grandfather of one, Strausman was an avid tennis player, chess enthusiast and Civil War buff — visiting all of the major battlefields from Fort Sumter to Appomattox Courthouse. Now 99, he continues to be an aspiring poet and potter.

Wondering

I wrote a poem many years ago
celebrating my happiness,
but never stopped wondering
what pure chance or minor decision
would have had major impact in my life

It is impossible to know the results
of taking the road more "traveled by"

Still, I wonder what happenstance
might have changed the course of my years
Would I be famous today? Richer, poorer?
Have more friends? Or none?
Be childless? Happy? Miserable?

Yet in these thoughts, realizing
I have been so fortunate, so blessed
"That then I scorn to change my state with Kings"

What If ?

There are so many "what ifs" in the world
which could have changed the course of history
"What if" Booth had been stopped on the stairs at Ford's
Theatre?
"What if" Germany had beaten us to the secrets of the atom?
"What if" Jack had not been killed? Or Bobby?
What would our world look like now?

"What if" I had not seen her
that day in August, almost a half-century ago?
I would not have met her, loved her, married her,
had children with her;
lived with her for 49 happy years,
watched our grandchildren grow

That "what if" might not have changed the world
But, it surely would have changed mine

Words

Can the meanings of words knock you for a loop
when you try to name animals in a group?

Is a prickle of porcupines with many sharp quills
better than a shiver of sharks to give you the chills?

Does a murder of crows seem more of a crime
than an ambush of tigers in the dark of nighttime?

Can ducks be a paddling and lions have pride
while otters romp on the outgoing tide?

Are convocations of eagles and parliaments of owls
wiser than cackles of hyenas — despite their frustrated howls?

Doesn't a lounge of lizards merit a scold of jays,
while a charm of finches brightens your days?

Saying a surfeit of skunks is very appropriate, I know;
but does a bloat of hippo weigh more than a crash of rhino?

I know wombats have wisdom and kittens pounce,
but can flutters of butterflies be weighed by the ounce?

If a wreck of seabirds is followed by a buzzards' wake
is a plague of locusts more than we can take?

Do rattlesnakes rhumba or squirrels scurry,
monkeys play in barrels
or buffaloes have obstinacy, thereby provoking quarrels?

If a leap of leopards and a pandemonium of parrots
easily comes to mind
are a squad of squid, unkindness of ravens or sneak of weasels
harder to find?

For a group of people can we use heroes of husbands
and wonder of wives
or giggles of girls, who every day bring much joy to our lives?

What did I save for the last and best of these wonderful words?
An exaltation of larks, describing a flight of beautiful birds

Woman

While the years may leave some trace,
time doesn't make a woman old
Though you may see its passage in her face,
look more closely and behold
A spirit who kept her youthfulness
with laughter and joy unspoken
She created her own happiness,
despite once having her heart broken
Shed tears she tried to hide,
she surmounted this sorrow
with family at her side
Looking forward to tomorrow,
soon love enriched her life
The once broken heart did mend,
beloved mother and wife
 — and, her husband's best friend
Youth can be wasted on the young;
youthfulness is a song unsung

The Real Genie

Walking on the beach yesterday
my feet hit something half-buried in the sand
I dug it out and said to myself:
I found the Genie in the bottle — and I will get three wishes
My first wish was for health for myself and those I love
My second wish was for world peace
My third was for wealth
I rubbed the bottle, but nothing happened
I was about to throw it away
when I noticed a folded paper inside
I fished it out, opened it up, and read:
Whoever finds this — I love you!
I imagined someone lonely, on a lonely beach,
reaching out with longing to an unknown
with those three simple words
This Genie didn't give me health,
or provide world peace,
but gave me the feeling that
I am immeasurably wealthy

25

Miracles

I do not believe in miracles
The burning bush, the loaves and fishes,
the parting of the Red Sea,
receiving the Ten Commandments,
are only fables dreamed up by men
Then I looked at the newborn baby
in the mother's arms
— and, I changed my mind

My Little Girl

We fell hopelessly in love at first sight
She was part of our life for sixteen years,
sleeping quietly at my side every night
Tiny, but an alpha among her peers
We left parties to hurry home to her,
but we never regretted it at all
Fourteen years passed in a pleasant blur
After she started to stumble and fall
we changed our lives to give her good care
When she no longer had much joy in life,
love made us do what we could hardly bear
We cried when she died, man and wife
When first seen she was as big as my fist
Grew to seven pounds — and is deeply missed

Picnic Ready

Teacher said: "On a picnic we will go"
They dressed for the weather and brought food
Everyone was happy; no one said, "No!"
Off they went with teacher in a fine mood
Susan said to teacher: "I have to go!"
"Go behind the tree, but your socks don't wet"
Ellen asked the same question, you know
and was given the same answer, you bet
John was next to be told behind the tree,
but was not warned about wetting his socks
— so the girls decided to look and see
They couldn't understand the paradox
What did they see but Johnny's wonderful trick
Sue said: "That's real handy for a picnic!"

Aging

Once they clutched
each other in the throes
of passion
Then, as they lay
exhausted, naked, sweating,
his hand often felt lovingly
for hers
Now, after so many years
together
their passion has subsided,
but their love has
increased
She watches him,
worried
that age-diminished
strength and balance
can cause him to
fall
He worries about her
happiness
after he has gone,
repeatedly telling her:
Life is for the living

Plurals

To be safe from snakes
a mongoose is what it takes
So I ordered one, but changed my view
— and decided to get two
Wrote in my letter: Please send two *mongooses*
But then I thought better — and asked for two *mongeese*
Which still didn't seem right, an error wanted to cover
After some thinking I write: Please send me a mongoose,
also please send me another
This made me think of plurals:
one intramural, two *intramurals*
Though more than one mouse is mice,
the plural of spouse is *not* spice
— although the thought is quite nice

Someday (2014, 2022)

The years go by
and old friends die
Jack and Al, Ben and Cy
Gene, with courage met his end
— and I have lost another friend

But for me death has no fears
I've enjoyed some golden years
Danced to a joyful tune,
seen the roses of many a June
Kept my word, paid my bills,
and survived my few ills

To those I will leave behind:
Remember, I was strong when I had to be
— and kind when I could be kind
I hope you'll not grieve too long,
yet still remember me

All things have their ends;
except love for family and friends
Friends and family, life's most precious things
My love for them will endure
when breath and life have taken wings

(Interlude)

Eight more years have flown by,
I have endured finally to see
the last of the old group die
— until there's none left but me

Harry was the last to go
He, Ernie, George, Pearl,
Ted, Celia, Herb and Marty
will not be at my 100th birthday party

I miss them and unnamed others
Yet, although nothing can replace a friend,
there is a grandchild's marriage to attend
And our first great-grandchild is on the way
Life is for the living, I say

The years have quickly flown by
and I have seen many old friends die
And I know someday,
though I trust, not soon,
so shall I

Time

Whether you count time by the century,
hours, seconds, B.C. or A.D.
time moves onward, doesn't show it,
brushing aside attempts to hurry or slow it
Whether you mark its passage by the pencil lines
you drew over your child's head
or the growth of the unborn fetus
or the pages in the books you read,
whether you dread or celebrate
the birthday that brings you closer
to the end of your earthly fate,
that emotionless clock will keep ticking
Whether the days bring you joy or woe,
today is always followed by tomorrow
The tree will be taller, your children will grow
Time brings happiness — and sorrow

No Regrets

I have lived many years
and done much
Still, I have many desires, which Father Time's
relentless clock, I regretfully believe,
will never allow me to achieve
The many books unread,
the plays I have missed
Some heartfelt regrets unsaid,
many beautiful girls *unkissed*
Much great art not glimpsed,
too many people not convinced
Yet it all comes down to this:
to see my children and their children,
to live long years with one I love,
to realize I have been so blessed,
that then I barely care about the rest

Your Love

Your Love
warms my
beating heart
more than you can know,
in ways which I cannot express
Your Love
sustains
me always
in all that I do,
makes every day a happy one
Your Love
also
enriches
many other lives,
shining like a star in the night
Your Love
denies
time's passage
and age's ravages,
keeping you lovely and youthful
Your Love
truly
gives my life
fullness and meaning
as our years together glide by

Signs of Youth

Driving a girl with *Dangerous Curves*
I read her my favorite traffic sign,
which said *Yield*
She told me I was on a
 Slippery Road to a *Dead-End*
— and said *Stop*
I wanted to *Keep Right*
and had the urge to *Merge*
So there was only *One Way* to go:
No Parking, No Passing;
Slow, *Beware of Children*

I Yam

I am a moonbeam shining in the daytime
I am the antithesis of everything
I am the know-it-all of ignorance
I am the wealth of poverty
— and a glutton of starvation
I am the truth of falsehoods,
the ugliness of beauty,
the resignation of hope
I am the indifference of love
I am the denial of acceptance
I am the treachery of allegiance
I am a blur of clarity, also a hill of valleys
I am a generality of specifics
I am the neatness of disorder,
a force of weakness
I am the importance of insignificance
I am the length of brevity
and the noise of silence
I am the evil of goodness,
the brilliance of stupidity
— and the humility of pride
Finally, I am the triumph of failure

I Wonder

I wonder where we will go
after fouling up the only nest mankind has ever known
I wonder how long we can continue to damage our lifeboat
before we sink
I wonder if we can travel to another planet and make it our own
I wonder whether any water there will be fit to drink
I wonder if we could clean up its polluted air
I wonder what we might find there
I wonder who stays here
I wonder
And,
I fear

Susan Aster Wallman

Ninety-two years young, Susan (nee Aster) Wallman was born and raised in Brooklyn and has lived on Long Island since 1965 — first on the South Shore in Baldwin and, since 1969, on the North Shore in Great Neck. Retiring from the work-a-day corporate world in 2015, Wallman joined Evelyn Kandel's poetry writing class. Trained as an actress at both Ithaca College and Adelphi College [now, University], Wallman acted with future *Love Boat* Captain Gavin MacLeod and had leading roles in productions in college and in summer stock and local theatre groups. Although theatre was her first love, she spent more than 60 years in business, during which time she and husband Irwin, who passed in 2017, raised their daughter Elisa, a social worker (and now mother of two), and son Robert, a graphic designer. She worked in advertising at both United Artists and Columbia/Epic Records; then for 34 years at McGraw-Hill, where she managed both the organization's corporate and foundation philanthropic programs focused on financial literacy, with strong support of nonprofit theatre and museums. During those years, Wallman made use of her poetry writing and "talent to amuse" (apologies to Noel Coward), often called upon to compose and perform celebratory verses in honor of senior management. She once met President Bill Clinton at an event — and, wrote a poem about it.

Marilyn's Mattress

Ah, you ask: Is what they say true?
My dears, *absolutely!*
Rated "Best New Box Spring Mattress of the Year" in 1953,
I was whisked away to a castle, Canada's Banff Springs Hotel,
to grace the bed of movie icon Marilyn Monroe
Oh my . . . how it pleasured me!
When folks are acting in a show, one tells them:
Break a Leg! for good luck
Alas, while filming the movie *River of No Return*
at nearby River Bow,
Miss Monroe broke her ankle!
Feeling quite yucky, Miss M curled up on me,
day and night
Never lonely though, her soon-to-be hubby number two,
Joe DiMaggio — yes, the baseball champ,
dubbed *Joltin' Joe* — stayed with her
They just gently cuddled;
no chance for hot and heavy loving
as Miss M lay in pain
As years went by many other guests staying at the castle,
some famous, some not,
had the pleasure of sleeping on me
One young vacationer I recall
had thrown her back out-of-whack while traveling
— and needed *me* for sleeping comfort
She came to be known years hence as *sanSu*
You may know her
Truth be told, now I've grown old,
I'm somewhat saggy in my middle
But in my heyday I was the absolute best,
supporting any size of guest; for a sleepy-time-stay
— or a roll in the hay!
And in my aging memories my thoughts
return from time to time
to my maiden voyage here in Banff
. . . and that maiden fair,
the very first to grace me:
Marilyn

33

Me and Pooh

(A Hum)
I am:
Susan, I'm Susie and I'm Suzy-Q
Some of you may take to calling me Sue
I am Susan-ba-du-zan
SuSu, Surele, Sooz
I am Suza-la-bella
and (would you believe!) Snooze
And here's a bit of *howdeedoo:*
a Philippine nurse flipped my name
— to *sanSu!*

[My Dad's response about names was a winner:
"Just don't call me late for dinner!"]

Here's more about me, though not the sum
— like Winnie the Pooh, I like to hum
I hum in my head, and even out loud,
though not very often when out in a crowd
Pooh's hums were little songs that he had written
I, on the other hand, usually am smitten
with words and with music that aren't my own,
but down through the years may all have been known
Sometimes my hum is merely a snatch;
sometimes a hum of all something will hatch
A hum-diddle-dum perches right on my psyche . . .
never forewarning of what the hum might be
But truly, once some little hum has just come to me,
I might say, in truth, that it's mighty good company!

Go Figure!

See how we go by in decades,
count out our ages by tens
Seems 'tis always been thus,
no need for a fuss
My, my, how they fly,
how they scurry on by . . .
to wit, thus:

See the sage centenarian,
nonagenarian,
octogenarian,
septuagenarian
All've passed sixty,
just after fifty,
moaned about forty,
tiptoed thru thirty,
thru twenty
and ten!
You dig?
I knew that you would!

Alive, but...

People said it was closed,
Family Fruit Farm store on Great Neck Road
Today I learn: It's open, still alive
Praise be the market gods!
Open, yes. But *not* the same wonderful owners:
hard-working Korean family, husband carefully
arranging produce and other items all around the store;
his little wife (what *was* her name) behind the counter,
ringing up my weekly stash, taking money
— and best of all, exchanging funny jokes with me,
her accent so strong I strain to hear
and chuckle politely as she explodes in laughter

So, these two naughty boys climb up a tree
Mother says: "Come down!" They don't
Father says: "Come down!" They don't
Parents call for Priest
Priest crosses himself and says:
"You come down from tree — or I'll kill you!"
Boys come down

Gone, the hard-working little lady and her husband
But not my memories of them on so many years
of Saturday merriment and fabulous fare,
shopping for my family
at their wonderful Family Farm

Shadorma Forma, Three Times I Conforma

Sad, so sad . . .
She sounded so sad on the phone
I told her some funny stories. *Voila!*
Her sad turned to glad

Do, Sue, do write a fun ditty about us
Yes? You will!
To read at our wedding? Yes!!
Wow! Do we love you!

Can't help it!
I stop a woman,
extol her
— all because
her gray hair is so gorgeous
I wish it were mine

Wait . . . They Will Come

The scene turns tender,
but troubling up on the silver screen
Unabashedly choked up, I'm quite tearful,
fully immersed in the sadness
of those actors / characters whose lives
— no matter, make-believe — are in pain,
which seemingly has traumatized me as well
Yet were my own world turning upside down,
or that of someone dear to me . . .
Where is my visible sorrow? Where are my tears?
Oddly, not in those moments
Sometimes though when least-expected, at some future moment,
I cry such mournful tears I hardly believe nor contain
As when the bugler playing taps as your coffin was carried
to your resting place, I cried such inconsolable tears
— seemingly, would never stop
And at an unexpected moment alone, caught up in a barely
remembered movie, some melody so tenderly sung beckons me,
caresses me, holds me . . . and I cry

A Legs Rap

(anti-Ode)

Hey what, look what, say what,
my legs
— see how the years have done you in!
What's happened legs to what you'd been?
Hey what, say what,
my lanky limbs
— what all that time has done to you

Let's face the truth, back in our youth,
you were no Betty Grable;
no pin-up, million-dollar gams
But, you were surely able

Not much that love had to do with it,
legs . . .
you were no glam wage earner
No prize, no *perfect pins*
Uh, uh . . .
You were no Tina Turner

Just fairly fine is what you were,
not twigs like Phyllis Diller
You slow-danced, *Charleston-ed, Lindy-hopped,*
— no tap, though, like Ann Miller

But these days, legs: you bruise, you wrinkle;
your ten extending toes, no twinkle
You partner with a walking cane
Your tingling's driving me insane!

Yet face it, legs. Long as we stay joined
and long as you're not bucklin',
legs: knock your knees
and swing your hips, rock 'n' jive
— and keep on truckin'!!

Ode to Nothingness

No cadence of poetic concept,
nada . . . no clue . . . gloms onto
this barren brain of mine,
in this seemingly interminable, endless night

No sprinkling of an inkling
showers my subconscious
Yet . . . what comes here?
Some thought, idea?
Poetic theme to dream upon, perhaps?

No . . . 'tis at best
some bestial nightmare,
nothing more

Begone! I say,
You ugly unwanted thing!

I long for friendly dawn
Surely the bright light of day
shall fill my dreary brain
with some desired poetic wonder

Therefore, resigned I am 'til then
— to lie here, deep in darkness,
my feeble barren brain, anxious, waiting
. . . altogether in the all-together

State of Grace

Don't you just love wordplay?
It's the best fun there is
Take the theological condition known
as *State of Grace,* for instance
What if, just what if, playing with those words
here in the U.S.,
was a small *state*, smaller even,

than *poor little Rhode Island,*
but an imposing state, nonetheless
— named *Grace!*
I think I might like to live in Grace,
with its sights and sounds and touch
and smells and tastes;
steeped in love,
magnificent mountains,
chirping of birds, pillow-soft flower petals,
aroma of gentle rain, sweet taste of honey
Where fear has no place, pain knows no entry,
love, given freely, touches everyone
Yes indeed . . .
I would like to live in such a state of Grace

Birth of a Notion

A word
intrudes
A phrase I heard
or one I said
Logical,
absurd
Frivolous,
solemn
Withdraws,
returns
Takes hold,
gains strength
Seeks rhymes,
roams free
Expands,
contracts
Flip-flops,
backs up
At last . . . stays put
Becomes
my
poem

Uncanny Happening

Mystified, why it was
I had such anxiety,
decided to stop in at
a little Asian cocktail lounge

Unaccustomed to frequenting
such a place, scanned the menu,
told the waiter:
I'll have a grasshopper cocktail
and sukiyaki on the side

Never had such a cocktail
Drank down the minty concoction in one gulp,
was drowsy before long,
with serious heartburn

Somewhat high and out of focus,
could make out on the opposite wall
a large impressionistic painting
of vivid yellow jonquils
— just before I zonked out!

Don't know how long that was,
but I woke abruptly:
Left the sukiyaki!
Left some cash!
Left the lounge!
And, in a nutshell:
Left with no high, no anxiety!

Pintimacy

I just adore my oval amber pin
in its surround of silver filigree
And men and women, both, admire it;
one quite unique admirer of all

Though many years ago, it's still so clear
At The New York Public Library
the corporation I worked for was sponsoring an
important event, and I was there with our staff
Ovation for the speaker ebbed, and then

I led him to our staff's reception line
He graciously shook hands with everyone,
including me, and as he did, it's true

Former President Bill Clinton
leaned toward me, and whispered low:
"I like that!" pointing to my dear amber pin,
the pin my husband Irwin had given to me
— reason for the gift now not so clear

Since then when praise is offered to my pin,
my mantra-like response is always thus
I lean in, intimately, and confide:
"My Husband, Bill Clinton . . . and *you!*"

Reverie at Dawn

I watch the sun each new day as moment to moment it peeps
through the small parting of window drapery in my bedroom
— and yet this new day I see myself back in a wondrous time
between sophomore and junior years of college, acting with a
summer stock company [one of my college pals there too,
Allan See (that being long before he would make
it big in show business, by which time he'd changed his name
to Gavin MacLeod)]
But, I digress, because I wanted to say I'd appeared in most
of the plays we put on weekly (having starring roles in a couple)
— but the week the company performed *The Hasty Heart*,
I worked crew as assistant to the lighting guy;
that time, that magical time, comes back to me now
as the sun lights up my bedroom and I see
the stage curtains draw apart, the set revealing
in pre-dawn darkness a makeshift Army hospital
deep in the jungles of Burma,
injured men not yet up (it's 1945, World War II is winding down)
and then slowly, ever so slowly, moment by moment,
I maneuver the electrical dimmer — creating, if you will,
the illusion of daybreak, of dawn, of the Sun
slowly peeping through the tall jungle trees,
lighting the bleak hospital room — and it is that *darkness-to-light*
that I, as if by *magic*, created . . . that in my dreamy reverie
magically lights up my yet un-played day today

JUDITH ZILBERSTEIN

A native of the Bronx, Judith Zilberstein was born at the Bronx Hospital in 1944 and graduated Bronx High School of Science. She earned a B.S. in Biology and an M.A. in Science Education from City College of New York, then traveled Europe and, getting married, honeymooned in Brazil and Argentina — her husband, from Buenos Aires. She worked as a medical secretary, as a laboratory specialist in an intermediate school in Spanish Harlem, as a research assistant for the New York City Rand Institute and taught at a psychiatric hospital, working with children who could not be maintained in a regular school setting due to behavioral problems and a variety of psychological disorders. Married for 51 years, Zilberstein has two children, two children-in-law and four grandchildren and among her world travels she has been to the Galapagos Islands, the Arctic and Antarctica, and a river cruise on the Danube from Prague to Budapest. She's even walked on a glacier in Alaska — drinking glacial water. It was on a sabbatical that she took up writing poetry. Retired since 2005, she enjoys Mahjong, Bridge and spending time with friends and family.

Armed and Dangerous

Your brain can be a lethal weapon,
source of the words that come out of your mouth
Words can kill a friendship, sever family ties, break hearts

Once said they cannot be unheard
An apology may assuage your guilt,
but cannot erase the scar left by a deep wound

Caution, your weapon is always loaded,
ready to fire at the merest provocation;
set to tear into your target

To avoid irreparable damage
caused by shooting your mouth off
think *before* you speak

The Age of Ists

My calendar is full
Lest you think I'm
a social butterfly,
let me tell you with whom
I am spending my time
There is the:
Allergist, Cardiologist, Dermatologist,
Gastroenterologist, Gynecologist, Orthopedist,
Ophthalmologist, Psychologist, Urologist
I could go on, but in the interest of saving
ink and paper I'll stop here
 In the good old days, Internists
or General Practitioners
took care of most health problems,
referring you to a specialist
when needed. Now, whenever you
voice a complaint, you are sent
to an *ist*
Note to self:
Unless you are in excruciating pain,
keep your mouth shut!

An Itty Bitty Ditty

Sing a song
all day long
You can't go wrong
when you sing a song

Yo, ho, here we go
Sing it high, sing it low
Sing it fast, sing it slow
Happier spirits you'll never know

Can't carry a tune,
so just croon
And sometime soon,
be happy as a loon

Don't like my ditty?
I think it's pretty
It makes me giddy,
when I'm in the city

Truth be known
you can write your own
You won't drone
if it's well-sown

Sing a song
all day long
You won't go wrong
if you sing a song

Rat-a-Tat-Tat

Hey, frightened little mouse,
come, come out of your house
We can play in the yard
That won't be so hard
Don't be so meek
We can play hide and seek

I can teach you how to shoot
That will be a hoot
We'll use my new AR-15
It's really keen
It will soon be our national gun
Come on, let's have some fun

Why am I aiming at you?
I'm a rat, that's what I do
I can shoot you in the heart
I can tear you apart
I can shoot you in the head
Rat-a-Tat-Tat
— you're dead

Metaphorically Speaking

My life is just a bowl of cherries
Oops, not original!
How's this?
My life is a spool of thread,
sometimes binding things together,
sometimes impossibly knotted,
sometimes unraveling
Nobody knows when the spool will run out of thread

My husband is my rock
Talk about your cliches!
My husband is the cozy blanket
I wrap myself in to feel loved,
safe, protected

My grandchildren are the light of my life
Not at all original!
My grandchildren are the music of my life
Their melodies are pure,
rich, and joyful

My family is a bowl of mixed nuts;
nuts are good for my health
Is there anything under our sun
that has not been said before?

Himself

I wonder why you say he's not himself today
I wonder who he is if not himself
I know he's not who he was, nor who he will be
But he is himself, now and always

I wonder if you can accept the man he is,
with glimpses of who he was
Can you embrace the present man,
grieve the loss of the man he was
and move forward
into uncharted territory

A Whale Tale

A whale swam close to our ship
when I was cruising the Arctic Ocean
He was rather chatty about his likes
and dislikes, though I had not asked
a single question

This is what he said:
*I am King of the Whales and will
teach you something that most
people do not know about us;
more specifically, about me*

*I don't like strawberries or grapes
I don't like to swim in rivers;
when compared to the ocean
I look like a balloon
the size of an ant*

*I would love to have hands
I could use the toaster or a grill
and have nice crisp food instead
of this soggy krill and the occasional
fish or squid; if I had hands I could
hold a fig and take dainty bites*

I would like to be a pilot, fly high
across the ocean and see the sights
I have heard so much about;
I would travel all over the world

Before I could say a word the whale
abruptly showed me his tail
and swam away, leaving me to wonder
if this was a dream or a tale told
to me by a very chatty whale

A Series of Unfortunate Events

Tooth extraction
Take antibiotic
Causes intestinal problem
Visit doctor
Blood tests
All normal
Problem continues
Back to doctor
More tests
Diagnosis: intestinal bacteria
Antibiotic
Weak from infection
Fall
See orthopedist
Broken ankle
Need surgery
Surgery scheduled
Go to hospital at 7 a.m.
Surgery canceled
Infection must clear
Week later, surgery
Metal plate, screws
Develop bronchitis
Antibiotics
Finally, feel better
Oh, mamma
Bad karma
What drama

47

Weather Head

There are days when I pop out of bed
The sun shines brightly in my head
The world is filled with vibrant colors
I think of all I have accomplished
I am optimistic
I am energized

There are days when I wake up
with dark clouds in my head
I see the world in tints of black
Want to pull the covers over my head,
stay in bed, think of all that I haven't done
and all that I should not have done,
even though I know it is not time well-spent

As a rule I don't stay in bed on the dark days
I get up, do as much as I can,
try to look forward to brighter days
On rare occasions, I stay under the covers,
avoid contact with anyone and anything;
close my eyes, sleep a dreamless sleep

My head knows the dark days won't last
There are many more sunshiny
days to look forward to
It knows to be grateful for what I have
To be thankful for being

Portrait

A portrait painted by
my sister hangs in my
living room, a sixteenth
birthday gift

I posed for the portrait,
was too antsy; finally
frustrated, my sister used
a photo instead

Looking through the artist's
eyes I see a girl with
an enigmatic expression
on an unblemished face

I do not treasure that period
in my life; I was an unhappy teen,
self-conscious, my face
. . . abloom with acne

I do treasure the portrait
painted so long ago; grateful to have
this gift that grows more precious
with each passing year

Good Indeed

Old woman
struggles to carry
groceries
In distress,
she attempts to catch her breath
— and puts her bag down
I offer
to carry her bag
She accepts,
though wary
We walk to her home, enter
her small apartment
She is safe
I put the kettle
on for tea
Steamy hot,
she drinks the tea gratefully
Feels warmth flow through her
Good feeling
from so long ago;
stays vivid,
warms the soul
Benefitted two
A good deed, indeed

Through the Pane

Through my kitchen window day is dawning
It is a fine winter morning
The sun rises
through a cloudless sky,
streams through
the bare-branched oaks;
blanches all it touches
It is hard to be downbeat
on such a glorious day
Yet, all it takes to bring on the blues
is a quick glance at any newspaper
So many disasters, so much
internal turmoil and political unrest
So many worries
Back to my kitchen window, where I see
the sun shining through the pane
Watch the children at play;
pray for better, kinder,
happier days

At the End of the Day

Ill will persists,
a potential smoking gun
The disproportionately vulnerable
are adversely affected by
differing views from people
who are shockingly ill-informed
and reckless; the guilty are facing
possibility of criminal charges
Possibility? Are you kidding me?
Where is the safety net?
We live in a time
of shocking concepts that enrage
— and alternative facts that incite
Can't we find something that works
and end this era of turmoil,
confusion, uncertainty
— and impending disaster?

Bitter Herbs

I think of Ilona
Especially, at the Passover seder
when we bless and eat bitter herbs

At one seder my grandfather passed
a sprig of symbolic bitter herbs
to each of us to bless and eat
Ilona refused,
said she had enough bitterness in her life
I didn't know what she meant

My mom told me Ilona and her family
were captured by the Nazis and sent
to a concentration camp;
she was ten, her family's only survivor
Near death, emaciated, dehydrated,
she begged her sister to look for water
— and never saw her again
Rescued by the Swiss Red Cross,
she was sent to live
with a family in America
She married my mom's cousin
I was her flower girl

History tells us how many people
were imprisoned, how many
perished at the hands of the Nazis
We will never know how many
people like Ilona were unable to have children;
how many future generations are never to be
How many survivors have nightmares
of torture they endured

Ilona was beautiful
Very petite, with dark hair, big blue eyes,
a dazzling smile — and, miraculously,
a wonderful sense of humor

Every Passover
when we eat bitter herbs
I think of Ilona

JOHN LANGE

John Lange was born in Chicago in 1931. Primarily, he has been a professional philosopher — that, having debated whether to become an Assyriologist. While acknowledging the thrills of deciphering cuneiform tablets having to do with grain deliveries to temples, philosophy won out. Lange has been a radio and film writer, the films with Photographic Productions, a unit connected with the University of Nebraska. He was also a Sergeant in the Army of the United States; a story analyst with Warner Brothers Motion Pictures; a technical editor and special materials writer in the rocket-engine industry with Rocketdyne, a Division of North American Aviation; and, eventually, a teacher of philosophy — first at Hamilton College in upstate New York, later at Queens College in the City University of New York. In college, Lange knew Dick Carson, brother of then-future *Tonight Show* legend Johnny Carson, and once spent an afternoon and evening with Johnny, who was working for station *KFAB* in Omaha, Nebraska. Among other things, Johnny Carson was a magician and ventriloquist — and he showed Lange tips on ventriloquism. Another time, Lange had a brush with Buster Keaton when the silent screen star happened in, secretly and unannounced, for a showing of *The General* on campus at the University of Southern California. As Lange recalled: "As I left the theater I passed Mr. Keaton, within an arm's reach. It is quite likely Mr. Keaton would not remember this, but I never forgot." A baseball pitcher, Lange once had a tryout with the Chicago White Sox. Told to put on 20 pounds and come back, Lange said recently: "I'm still working on that."

Litany in Praise of Ideology

You are the straitjacket of the mind
You are the chain we cannot see,
which we do not know we wear
You are the penitentiary within which we think ourselves free
You bless the march of lemmings to the sea
You are the exoneration of the assassin
You wear the mask of God

You are the sound of the guillotine doing its work
You commend dupes singing in fires you have kindled
You are the contented quiet of the bombardier,
the guiltless crack of rifles,
the innocent whistle of falling bombs
You are the song no decent siren would deign to sing

You are the sugar-coated tablet of social cyanide
Sometimes you are modest and benign,
a mouthful of cheese doodles, packaged as philosophy
You cater to those who enjoy the taste of blood
You are a merchant, selling the wine of power,
a dealer hawking the drug of hate
You are fond of cemeteries
— and, sell flowers to decorate graves
In the ashes, your aftertaste is bitter

You exude a pleasant odor, as does the Venus Fly Trap
You are the perfume masking the stench of greed,
the stink of burning flesh
You are well-advised to remain downwind,
lest your prey suspect your presence

You are the blanket of snow in the blizzard,
in which one may comfortably sleep, and die
You are the anodyne of conscience
You are the best of puppet masters;
the puppets do not feel the strings
You bait the hook that seeks souls

Spare us the pain of thought
Rescue us from finding our own way
Save us from ourselves
Who will save us from you?

The Penguin

It was upon a midnight dreary,
while I pondered, weak and weary,
that I heard a tapping, a rapping, a banging,
a clanging at my kitchen door
That is most-likely why I put aside my volume of forgotten lore
At this hour no honest person could be about,
but nonetheless I dared look out
I looked into the stygian night, but nothing was in sight
I would close the door and turn my back,
but a small webbed foot was in the crack
A penguin waddled in and hopped atop my Frigidaire
It was not clear what he was doing there
"Butter Brickle," said the bird
What might these arcane words impart?
How can I convey the terror which seized my heart?
"Butter Brickle," said the bird
One thing I was sure I knew;
in Nassau County such birds were few
Geese many, but of penguins hardly any
"Butter Brickle," said the bird

This visitation was not here by invitation
It gazed upon me with a look imperious;
I was pretty sure that it was serious
Beware, begone, out of my sight;
I could call 911, as is my right
I was shaken to the core
The penguin said "Butter Brickle"
— and nothing more

I whistled for my guard dogs two, fierce pit bulls each,
a lesson the bird to teach
They soon showed up, each dangerous since a pup
I was sure a little growl would dismay the fearsome fowl
The penguin looked upon the dogs with eyes of fire
They whimpered and decided to retire
I supposed they had some reason;
perhaps it was the season for canine treason

Surely it was not mortal, what came that night past my portal
Had it sprung from some noxious, infernal, mystic crater
— to perch atop my refrigerator?

What did the eerie words portend?
Perhaps the world was about to end?
Was it devil, demon, wraith, or ghost?
I feared I might soon be toast

To understand you, I have vainly tried;
tell me what you mean, I cried
Your words are deep;
tell me the secret they keep

If you were smarter
you'd listen, for a starter
I will tell you what I mean
I want ice cream

Clocks

Clocks are liars
They pretend to tell time but they don't
Time does not get told
It doesn't even listen
They change but time doesn't
It has been claimed that time passes
This seems to be an error
It is things that pass
Not time
It just sits there and watches
It doesn't go in only one direction
It doesn't go at all
It has no steering wheel
It has no handles
Time touches us, but we can't touch time
That hardly seems fair
What if we could touch time?
What would we do with it?
But what if clocks invent time?
The sneaky bastards
Then, all bets are off
Besides, what clock do we use?
Pick a clock?
Pick a thousand clocks?
One time per clock?
It's not easy, manufacturing time

Why Economics is Called the Dismal Science

There is not enough to go around
And if there were, folks would want more
And then again, right then, again
there would not be enough to go around
Barracudas are not kind to small fish
Nature gave the cobra venom

The merry-go-round spins
while the horses starve

There is only so much waterfront property
On the top of the hill there is room
for only one house
Leo Durocher, Dodger skipper,
might be right
Nice guys finish last
Pollyanna is perplexed
Sharks and crocodiles survive

The merry-go-round spins
while the horses starve

Solutions are easy
Swift had one for the Irish
Nuclear cleansing is a possibility
Bacteriological warfare might work,
super plagues humbling the Black Death
Compassion regularly falls short

The merry-go-round spins
while the horses starve

On Serving the World

I can't dance
I can't sing, either
Thus, my act
of kindness
is to neither dance nor sing
Thus, I serve the world

Migrations: With High Hopes For the Space Industry

Archaeological evidence makes clear,
and records attest,
in cuneiform, hieroglyphics and such,
barbarians are on the march
It's nothing new

History may lack themes,
but it has its habits
In the book of the past
no chapter is more clear
Barbarians are on the march

Let the heavy-wheeled wagons roll
Let the bodies be painted,
the omens taken,
the arrows feathered,
the axes sharpened
Note the smoke
Hear the cries
They are on the march again

The tapestries of time are dark
The threads of history are dipped in blood

Outward, ho!
The universe or nothing
With luck there will always be more progress
Let us hope for the best
There will always be another planet to destroy

One Night on KOLN

Radio:
Late news, a ship sank
Woman called;
spouse on ship
I told her: "No casualties"
"Thank you," she whispered

57

On Painting Invisible Fences

There was this famous superhero
who was invisible,
but only when no one was looking
This reminded me
of the famous philosophical problem
of the invisible fence
If you have not heard of it,
that is all right
I just made it up
The invisible fence, of course,
is easily noticed,
if one bumps into it
Poets are good at bumping into invisible fences
It is one of those things,
like putting out the garbage,
which they do well
Poets paint invisible fences,
making them show up
We might not know there was a fence there,
or a forest or a world,
or a feeling or a thought,
if the poet did not paint it
That's one of the poet's jobs,
making visible what was invisible
They call attention
to what we did not know was there before
Invisible fences show up when painted,
unless you use invisible paint
Then they don't

Fortress

I am a fortress with no gate
I do not know who is on the battlements
Why is there no gate?
I am a locked box, with no key
I am an animal, recalling a vanished ancestor,
perhaps one so terrible he is best forgotten
I am a secret text,
recorded in a lost language,
never to be deciphered

On the Occasional Ineffectuality of Erasers

It was 10 p.m.
The classroom was empty
The classroom was dark
The blackboard was innocent
It did not complain
It accepted the weight
of several chalk particles with ease
The chalk particles continued to do
what chalk particles do best,
cling to a slate surface
A passing mouse had a good deal
— no cats and several careless students,
liberal with donations
The custodian entered the room,
and turned on the light
He erased the board,
but he could not erase the poem
It had only been stopping by
The chalk particles did not even know
a poem had visited them

A Song We Sometimes Think We Hear

Odysseus stopped the ears of his men
They could hear nothing
They had no chance
They could not listen
Ithaca's king determined it so
Himself he had lashed to the mast
He heard the song and lived
That was cheating, in a way
He heard the song,
but declined to pay its price
Odysseus was always a wily rogue
Recall the wooden horse,
its belly filled with Argives
I do not think the sirens would object, not really
Were it not for Odysseus we would not know
there had been a song,
a song we sometimes think we hear

On the Possible Utility of Keeping Secrets

I do not know myself
I am a stranger to myself
Ask Dr. Freud
I am not sure I want to know myself
I am not sure I would like myself
Socrates recommended knowing oneself
I wonder if he really gave it a shot
Did he have six years of intensive psychoanalysis?
Would he have been pleased with what he saw?
Is not the knower always hidden from view?
Maybe it is best that way
Not all questions need be answered
Perhaps not all questions should be answered

International Tensions in the Barnyard

It is a well-known fact that dogs
have accents and nationalities
From a dog who speaks English,
you will hear *bow-wow*
— or, sometimes *woof-woof* or *arf,*
depending on the part of the country
A German dog comes up with *wow-wow*
and one that's Polish with *how-how* and so on
It's pretty much the same with roosters
The English rooster says *cock-a-doodle-doo,*
the French one *cocorico*
and the German one *kikeriki*
Needless to say, this sometimes causes problems,
particularly in border areas
Territorial disputes and border crossings are common
Dogs are unsure of who to bite or what to fetch
Hens are puzzled, too
Shall they lay English, French or German eggs?
International law founders
The United Nations is helpless
It is not clear what is to be done
Luckily, Fido and Chanticleer
lack nuclear weapons
— as of now

Pervasive Artifact 127.B

It is a long time since the *bâton de commandement*
of the Upper Paleolithic Period,
with its round hole,
was thought to be a symbol of status or power
We put that aside when we discovered
contemporary primitives still using it
to straighten arrows
Something similar may pertain to Pervasive Artifact 127.B
Examples abound
Consider the Island Culture of Large Neck,
accessible now due to the diminution of radiation
The typical object is flat and octagonal,
for the shape of the Earth and its eight corners
The surface is red,
most likely denoting war and blood sacrifice
On this surface are four mysterious symbols
The symbols are white
One theory suggests that this stands
for decency, fairness, purity and innocence
Another theory has it that this stands
for persecution, tyranny, and oppression
In any event, the artifacts are numerous,
and commonly located
at the intersection of streets and roads,
where people would naturally gather
Their political, social, and religious significance,
while unmistakably momentous,
remains unclear
It remains one of the great unsolved mysteries
of anthropology

Occupying a Position of Advantage

I think the universe is mysterious
I am not alone in this
I have much company
The universe does not know it is mysterious
That puts us one up on the universe

Sheila Saferstein

Sheila Saferstein blends interests in the liberal arts in her lyric and narrative poetry. An Adjunct Lecturer of English Communications at New York Institute of Technology for 23 years, she taught Secondary School English for a decade at Port Washington Paul D. Schreiber and North Shore High School on Long Island. She was a guest lecturer at the Hofstra University Art History Department and the Brandeis University Club, where she presented Homer's *Odyssey in Greek Vase Painting*, and aboard the Cunard Queen Elizabeth 2 — where she presented *Interpersonal Communications and Art*. For years she was a judge for Long Island school poetry competitions at the Walt Whitman Birthplace, as well as being Poet Presenter of the Year in Manhasset. Sheila has sung music from the *American Songbook* at Juilliard and the 92nd Street Y and been a member of the New York Choral Society. Her rhythmic poetry is often based on allusions to classical mythology. She has been published in PPA Literary Journals and in the Nassau County Poet Laureate Society Review and studied with Nassau Poet Laureate Evelyn Kandel, as well as with Nikki Giovanni, Marie Howie, and Maxwell Wheat.

Shade

White not insulted,
never green with envy, red with rage
— though, seldom deemed a color
Nicknamed *shade,*
she absorbs all light around her
A white dwarf star, like pale efforts of a step-sister,
she lacks luminosity
Likened to the essence of milk filling the bottle of a baby,
to fresh snow fallen many winter nights before dawn,
to strands of pearls circling the throat
of a beauty enhancing her grace;
to the proud breast of an Arctic penguin,
to the royal robe of a Florentine Medici,
to ruffled trains trailing bridal gowns,
to the edges of ocean whitecaps,
tinkling sounds of Steinway keys,
white marble columns of the Parthenon
crowned in a riot of colors
— blue, green and red — worn away
by the soothing hands of time

Medea

Shedding notes of flaming embers
(*NEW YORK MAGAZINE opera criticism*)

Cherubini set to music Euripides' *Medea*
created opera's darkest colors:
shards of fiery crimson violin strings
pierce the hall;
soprano's throat-choking,
most-shrill screams empty souls
Medea's blinding rage,
ember-glowing horrors, her most-cruel murder,
revenge for her husband's infidelity
Medea's bloodiest eyes, hands smeared,
gown stained with babies' blood
Medea in all-consuming revenge
for her husband's infidelity

Ode to Antiquity

(After viewing the Metropolitan's Greek and Roman Gallery)

I long to touch
his white marble body
lying cold in an Olympian grave
awaiting my caress
centuries of civilization

I long to taste
flowing libations, sweet wine, water,
sip of milky rivers
from the rim of his funerary vase,
outpourings of a grieving wife

I long to hear
Apollo's lute, Muses' thunderous chorale,
ripples of Graces' laughter;
their polyphony from the heights of Parnassus,
as he and I prance off Homer's pages

I long to smell
happiness again, spicy scents of festivals,
pungent grapes grown in sun-drenched vineyards;
savor gods' honeyed ambrosia,
dripping from my lips

I long to see
from my aerial perch below Elysium
lithe fingers of the Peloponnesus
— in flight this time,
not in fancy

Of Me I Sing

Give me a role I could kill!
No soprano note I did not fulfill
Always auditioned! Never refused!
My life suffused
A little Puccini, Porter, Gershwin,
Berlin, Gilbert & Sullivan, too, all thrill
My trills of *Nutcracker,* all true
Holy songs, Christian and Jew

American Songbook, my favorites — I be so bold
Carousel, Oklahoma, Kiss Me Kate
I'd be loving them always; I'll sing along
Sinatra's songs, Ella's blues; truths be told
Lincoln Center, Broadway, Uptown, Down; my favorite haunts
Never in the ranks of Barbra, Celine, Carly; their voices taunt
Find me in company on many a site, like a lemming,
I promise you there's Renee Fleming
I shared my grandest dream, becoming like her
She retorted:
A career in opera her mother never, ever supported!
What show biz stars, their roles have I missed?
Like Piaf, my idol Renee, regrets:
We all have *quite a few*

Moonlit Memories

"In the Still of the Night
As I gaze through my window
At the moon in its flight
My thoughts all stray to you . . . "
— Cole Porter

Moonlight illumines
sailboats and skiffs;
sandy shores shine
across the bay

Dreams of grand homes
to make our own
many years ago,
when you were small

Moonlight illumines
moorings, anchorages;
awaiting late,
returning crafts

Filled with seafarers,
far away ports;
until you were grown,
owned your own barque

Life Lessons

Daddy's mantra comforted me:
Everything will be all right,
he whispered
I would glance inward;
remembered this essence
My tightened muscles relaxed

Back then, I believed
Hold on, Sheila;
wind your arms around my neck
As we torpedoed through mountainous ocean waves,
I believed

One beautiful June,
as we walked down the aisle
my arm looped through his
Everything will be all right
I still believed

In too few years
my husband, our son's father,
lay mortally ill; I quavered to believe
my Daddy's once-comforting voice
How could everything so wrong be all right?

Season's Changes

Golden leaves, like glittering coins,
swirl in chilling autumn winds,
gleam on sunlit hills now brown,
carpet soon snow-covered ground

Awaiting season's changes

Flocks of birds leave familiar places
to southern climes together fly;
are fledglings strong enough
to weather so many unfamiliar spaces?

Awaiting season's changes

Many trees seem to lose their strength,
droop in sad farewell to Mother Nature
Her defacements yet wholly unknown;
they understand she'll bring
next year's replacements

Awaiting season's changes

Squirrels scurry, carry nuts to savor
winter's meals in preparation;
furry bears, hedgehogs;
snails carry their shelters most-protective

Awaiting season's changes

Your Gifts

(Homage to Billy Collins)
I need no material gift,
no reason to cross,
strand over strand,
again and again,
until my lanyard is complete
Language of your presence,
your sacrifice of time,
speak to me

I read between the lines of our lives,
accept your deeds in purest love
I will not ever press for words,
misinterpret your intentions,
look for hidden meanings
Your willingness and generosity
are clear

If only I say a word,
whatever I think I need,
you'll leap and bound across my gate,
ever-ready to repair, replace, rearrange,
whatever claims attention
— however long tasks take
Your precious gift of time
makes my home right again

Curiosities

Oh my! What do I see?
Pairs of words,
seemingly having no connectivity
Until, after some research,
I play lost and found,
pair them with my thoughts most-profound
Grapes flourish near riverbeds,
I learn, thrive in dampness;
images swirl 'round my head
Fruits of the vine,
doused in Rhone's waters,
become sweetest wine
Now, what do I see
paired in whale *and* strawberry?
Look at shapes more closely;
it is most apparent fruit's shape has hump,
like this largest animal of the sea
Reversely, they do not share the colors strawberry;
either grey or black,
they do not share the slightest fleck
My search goes on – ant and balloon,
symbolism of the two
Cosmic imagery of inflated balloon
pairs ant, imagine creeping 'cross infinity
Now, toaster now hand ,
no similarity does exist, you say
Except, I persist! You'd better pray!
When appliance you need most,
self-reliance — watch that heat!
Do not be burned, pay attention!
Your hand might soon become toast
Finally, you ask, a pilot and a fig?
Now, do not become a prig!
At first, you might think fruit on tree
Fig might just be an abbreviation for *figure*
All pilots might agree
if you don't follow each and every
aviation chart every outline,
you might just end up
twisted down a vine

Cleanse

(Homage to W. S Merwin, *After the Voices*)

Getting round to forgetting,
need to purge my place
of quiet, inner voices
Feng shui, *my* mantra;
declutter, harmonize my soul
— too much space still inhabited by sounds,
need room to breathe
 Resolved to abandon all doodads;
discard broken, tick-less, timeless clocks,
unwatered, crying, withered plants,
out-dated calendars, stacked harsh reminders
— inscribed with sorrow
Must forget time, I am no pup;
my face like cracked mirrors,
each and every tooth like chipped teacups
Plates, bowls, expect memories of meals;
on-coming rains like tears
Earthly love's footsteps, passions' rising fires;
not quite over these elements
I will avoid memories, attach symbols to entanglements,
court silence, declutter haunting inner voices

Gone

Grandma came to Port Washington in 1912
from the Lower East Side
Met by uncle, drove his horse and cart to the train station,
traveled down the dirt road now known as Main Street
to his rooms above the tailor shop
Grandma, Uncle; horses, cart, dirt road
Gone, gone. All are gone
Visit the past, view the mural hanging behind the tellers at
Citibank
Sites we came to know so well; Brother's Market Fish Store
Gone, gone. All are gone
Sude, the jeweler. Please, repair my watch, my ring
Italian restaurant; now, Asian shoe shop
Gone, gone. All are gone
All, in time, are gone

69

Closets are Not to Store Tangibles

They keep alive the most intangible, treasured, memories
My Japanese Kimonos
— one short, my favorite often worn, hanging near
my shower door; the other, ankle-length long —
both black satin, woven on the same loom,
embellished with pink cherry blossoms, mums
Forever a treasure to hang in the darkness
of my closet, hardly ever worn;
never worn-out memories of my journey to Tokyo,
a visit with my dear son, during his college years
I'll never let go of either: treasured robes, cherished memories
Nearby in my bedroom closet,
a trunk filled with precious memories,
hangs an emerald green satin jacket
— a garment that may have been worn by Marlene Dietrich,
star of a movie now nameless
I am saddened to think it had been completed
last of a three-part suit;
skirt of burgundy, blouse of rust,
purchased for my marital trousseau
Silver earrings, set with green stones;
I purchased at a flea market a belt to match
Treasures lost during my many moves,
a memory brings joyous tears to my eyes

My Poem May Be a Hit of Mythic Proportions

Are you expecting one great story?
Our future is unpredictable;
we can pay it a visit
Doomsday is extremely nigh;
we've no plans to travel
I have many epiphanies a day: see experiences in new ways,
have insights that change my understanding
Later, I'll go to the library to research pickleball
Do people really change?
Can conversation save our souls?
What are the big ideas?
Billy Collins noted:
"You have to be interested in the playfulness
of poetry to want to keep writing it"

My Metaphorical Musings on Seasons

Winter doldrums aptly named
My moods darken, heart constricts
I struggle not to freeze like nearby ponds,
where geese slip and slide stay alive
on resident surface
Spring blossoms promise me hope;
twigs sprout, bulbs yearn to burst their secrets,
fill the air with fragrance
I await my May birthday
Summer speaks of permanence,
sky-blinding translucent light,
when nature like me gives birth
to this season's regenerative powers
Fall's transient colors;
deception reminds us we may renounce mortality
Illusion of permanence
What does does not endure?

Land of Enchantment

New Mexico, I would go
Territories: Apaches; Navajo, too
High, forested mountains, cold alpine climes;
warm lower arid spaces — deserts, cacti, all abloom
Fertile valleys of picturesque Rio Grande,
where I, like *Ozymandias,* might stand
Oversee this vast wilderness,
my powers, unlike his, undiminished;
where ranchers yet oversee herds of cattle
— Los Alamos, long before the doom of atomic battle
But, it is one doorstep I wish most to venture,
that of Georgia O'Keefe, modernist painter
Settled in Santa Fe, amidst her youthful great beauty,
fled East to West to live her best life
after the strife of separation
from her love, photographer Stieglitz
She painted New Mexican landscapes,
giant canvases of colorful petals
in museums now known
Fame, her world become materially renown

71

HATTIE ABBEY

One of the first Jewish children born in the historic Alice Weiss Maternity Hospital in Budapest, Hungary, post-World War II, Hattie Abbey was hidden by her parents under a blanket, mouth taped shut, as her family fled hyperinflation and Soviet occupation in 1946. She lived in a displacement camp in Germany, traveling en route in the same cattle cars used to carry victims to camps during the Holocaust. As a child she learned Hungarian, Yiddish, German, English and French — English being her fourth language — and arrived at Ellis Island in New York Harbor aboard the transport U.S.S. General M.B. Stewart in June 1951 after a harrowing trek that included being alone on deck, hidden in fear under a bench, during an Atlantic storm. She was five. She lived in the Bronx, later attended Great Neck South High School on Long Island, graduated Queens College cum laude and with special honors in earning her Master's Degree in Education at Hofstra University. A retired special education teacher, she was co-owner of the pre-school *A+ for Kids* in Great Neck. Her poetry has been published in local newspapers, as well as in the anthology *A Celebration of Poets: Showcase Edition 1999*.

Who Am I ?

I am a child who has
seen too much,
viewed things I cannot unsee,
suffered unkind words
Who am I?
I am a lover of humanity,
a suppressor of fears,
a keeper of stress
Who am I?
A creator of poems,
an admirer of words,
a head full of thoughts
Who am I?
Less than I want,
more than I have,
all that I believe
Who am I?
A work of art,
never completed,
looking for
a happy ending

Silence is Deadly

Latch-key child,
no one inside
Alone with concern,
until parents return
Feel like choking,
words unspoken
English unknown,
don't have a phone
TV on,
makes me feel calm
Until this day,
that's still my way

Nothing but Skeptics

Creedmoor State Hospital, 1964
Team meeting, discussion:
Six-year-old Johnny G., Autistic
Team members: psychiatrist, psychologist,
medical doctor, teacher
— and me, a nineteen-year-old
occupational therapy assistant

Language development team reports:
"Grunts, groans and screams"
I report: "Speaks in short phrases"
They all laugh
No one has ever heard Johnny speak
I beg them to listen
No video cameras,
my heart pounding
How do I defend my findings?

I tell them I have been working with him for weeks
I made a connection, using his favorite foods,
constant repetition and rewards

How did I know his favorite foods?
Spoke to his mom on Visiting Day

Nothing but skeptics

My husband owned a 35-pound Wollensak tape recorder
He carried it to the room
Johnny spoke: "More Cocoa Puffs!"
"Beans please!" "More bacon!"
"Mama!"

After sheer frustration I was vindicated, my integrity restored
Mom so pleased she had a Mass in my honor at her church
Guess she didn't know I was Jewish
She later wrote a book with a chapter
dedicated to my work with Johnny

Feels good when the underdog wins!

My Mother Came to Me

My mother came to me!
MY MOTHER CAME TO ME!
It was real! It was real!
MY MOTHER CAME TO ME!
I opened the bathroom door;
my eyes opened wide
I wanted to scream, to call my husband;
no sound would eject
There she stood in ghostly gray,
her kind eyes slightly glazed,
looking straight at me
I grabbed her hand;
her tough, strong hand,
that worked so hard all her life
I put my arms around her,
held her oh so tight
It was different than a dream: genuine, authentic;
nothing like I'd seen before
She came to console me!

My Purpose in Life

A teen,
mistreated by classmates;
school guidance teachers,
who didn't notice
A teen, who felt small
in a school so big
A town, so educated;
kids, so rich
I never fit in
I wanted to be a teacher
School said I couldn't;
future husband
said I could
Purpose accomplished:
Graduated with honors;
owned my own school
A life, fulfilled

Color Me Sad

When I was a child I loved to view
a box of crayons, oh so new
Tapered points, colored bright
What could be better? What a delight!
Imagination spurred me to sketch,
large white paper I went to fetch
A portrait of MLK I drew
The night of his death my fingers flew
The Fourth of April, Nineteen-Hundred-Sixty-Eight
I was unaware of what I'd create
A portrait I had never done,
it came from my heart to everyone
My heart breaks each and every year,
for I left it behind in school, I fear
When I think back it makes me cry
Each MLK Day, I give a big sigh

Buzz Off

The biggest fly I ever saw
came buzzing in through our front door
For days, he swooped around our house;
could not get rid of that dirty louse
Diverting the fly with *The New York Times,*
we were aiming for a murderous crime
Darting here and darting there,
that damn fly was everywhere
With complete frustration
I went to the store
to buy a fly swatter
"Please work, I implored"
We're swinging and slamming,
to no avail
When cornered in the bathroom
we could not fail
I stepped in the tub, opened
the window wide,
I shooed him out that orifice
with tremendous pride!

Obsolescence: The Pencil

We live in a world
of instant gratification
What chance does a pencil have?
A pencil from which
words flow like Niagara Falls;
rushing, to express a dream
The simplest of linear markings,
need no WiFi or internet
to perform its magic;
skipping across the page,
with strength and determination
How long will she be around?

Prose Poem Grows

Sitting on the beach, lazily gazing at the dunes
My toes snuggling that soft, yet gritty, feeling
Suddenly, I stretch my legs and push a smooth object
along the surface of the sand
I bend over to examine my find
It was a glass bottle, the kind ships are
often ensconced in,
cozily resting at the bottom
It was empty, just waiting
to be filled with words of wisdom
Thoughts whiz by like bunnies on Easter Sunday
I scribble a series of sentences
My heart starts to pound;
I toss the vessel vehemently into the Long Island Sound
The bottle finds itself in the
Intra Costal Waterway
under my Hallandale Beach window
There, on the terrace, stands my husband
"Come up sweetheart," he says
"I want to dance with you!"
I look down at my phone
and the date is
December 16th, 2019
MY BIRTHDAY!

An Old-Timer's Rap

When you bought appliances
back in the day
you knew they would last
— 'til you gave them away
I got a blender in 1968,
which still continues
to chop . . . and grate
When you got a phone
from the company
it never broke
— bet your money
My toaster I got
when I first wed,
it crisped and popped
— that's what I said
It lasted more than 25 years;
when I think back,
it brings me to tears
Must have had 10 since then,
my friend;
their life begins
— and, quickly ends
Companies were proud
of what was made
in the U.S.A.
Things made to last
— 'til your dying day
Today's products
become obsolete
before you send an e-mail
— or receive a Tweet
Calling and speaking
to someone alive,
not pushing buttons
from 1-to-5
It was a person
you spoke to
who wanted to help

and cared about you;
your questions answered,
'til you were satisfied
— no listening to ads,
until your head fried
While some new devices
make progress good,
sometimes things were better
back in the old neighborhood

Our Symbol of Freedom

A symbol of freedom standing high,
reaching upward to the sky
Eagerly waiting to be seen
by myriads of immigrants
— to fulfill a dream
Seven rays to symbolize
seven continents and seven seas
To shed her light of liberty,
so we can live with ease
America, a melting pot;
all wait to pass her doors,
anxious faces hoping . . .
to set foot upon her shores
Our statue, tall and beautiful,
so full of inspiration;
drew people from around the world
with anticipated fascination
They helped to make our country,
what it is today;
a symbol of freedom for all the world
— that's how we want it to stay
The words above
flow from within;
they come from one who knows
— for of the many
who came to this land,
I was one of those

Our Small House Grows

I am the culmination of a brave people
The strength of those who came before
lives within me
The hope of a better future lives
in my grandson
He will carry on the love, the knowledge
— and the burden
My mother's mother died in childbirth;
my mother's father carried on
He raised a family
with his new spouse and children
As the years passed the Holocaust erased
many of my loved ones' ability
to pass on their strength, knowledge
— and love
My parents lost their mothers and fathers,
siblings and other family members;
they were brave enough to escape
with infant me in tow
No money or belongings;
no one in America to help them
What strength they showed
They spoke no English
Yet, they flourished,
building a business
— becoming American citizens
I am grateful for what they did
to better my life
Moving from country to country
I not only learned to speak,
but by five years of age
I was on my fourth language
First in my family to got to college;
graduated cum laude, Queens College,
then to Hofstra University
In free. And, out with honors
My grandson carries generations
of strength, knowledge
and love
— from where our small house
will grow!

Validation

Writing about my past . . .
memories bombard my mind
Sitting on an older man's lap,
his hands wandering where
they should not go
on a seven-year-old girl
A religious man; a man of the cloth

Did it really happen?
It was so long ago

Never had a grandpa;
the Holocaust took that possibility
from me
Did not understand the inappropriateness
of his subtle actions — reading a story,
softly, gently, near my ear
How could this be wrong?
Thought never entered my mind
until I was 40
Circumstance led me to tell
my parents

Did it really happen?
It was so long ago

Just this week we had dinner
with friends
We were discussing child abuse
by Priests and Rabbis
with our friend, a well-known
sociologist
When my situation surfaced,
I received validation
Dr. Helmreich told us that
the Jewish press stated
that a Rabbi was arrested
for molesting
seven-year-old girls

It really *did* happen
— so very long ago

LILA EDELKIND

Lila Edelkind is a true New Yorker: born, bred and educated in New York City schools and Brooklyn College, her career as an educator spanning 34 years in the public school system. An early childhood teacher, Edelkind incorporated the British Infant School model and literacy approach into her methodology, connecting art and language. Recognized by the United Teachers Federation for "Write to Read," a program she developed to teach reading and writing skills by having students write, illustrate, and construct books to add to their class library, Edelkind became a workshop presenter for the New York City Writing Project at Lehman College. Later, she expanded work as a staff and curriculum developer, serving as director of programs for gifted and talented children, as well as administrator of grant-funded programs. She coordinated implementation of The Reading Recovery Program and was recognized by the NYU Teacher Training Staff. Career highlights included serving with the NYC Ballet and NYC Opera Education Advisory Committees and working with The Johns Hopkins Center for Talented Youth. Upon retirement, Edelkind took voice and acting lessons at Astoria ArtHouse and joined Theatre By The Bay NY — designing stage sets, crafting props, serving as administrator of its website and performing in a myriad of musicals. During the pandemic, Edelkind immersed herself in virtual learning — taking film, literature, knitting and Yiddish classes and writing poetry with Evelyn Kandel.

Dear Denial

Dear Denial,
Well old friend, it seemed I wouldn't
be able to hide from you any more
The writing task at hand forced me to open
a door I thought I had sealed off

You have been my cloak of protection,
my shelter from trials and tribulations
You have shielded me from truths I preferred not to see,
drumbeats I preferred not to hear
You handed me rose-colored glasses, whispered in my ear
that there was nothing to fear

You sent distractions to shift my focus,
to blur the thoughts that might lead to despair
You enabled me to lie to myself, just enough to take the edge off
— to help me keep going
when there was a threat that I might fold inward
as grief hovered too close

The process of writing these letters
offered me a key, urged me to open the door,
step over the threshold; to pry open the dust-covered chests
that held disturbing thoughts from many years ago
I know they are filled with the questions I failed to ask,
the actions I failed to take, the resolutions
that will never come to pass

Perhaps I can rely on you again
to tell me I'm being a drama queen;
that I should let sleeping dogs lie
If I turn around now and re-lock that part of my mind,
I can prove that you are still looking out for me
— that your powers still work
And I'll be in denial once more

With hesitant gratitude,
I remain yours

Lila

I'm in a State

I am in a frenzied state
for which I will just
state my case:

A state of confusion
about our Union
A state of consternation
about our Nation

A state of despair
for those who don't care
A state of emergency
for the lack of urgency

A state of anxiety
for those who spout piety
A state of concern
for those who won't learn

A state of mind
in which someday I'll find
a state of being
— to enlighten my seeing

A rational state
will return to negate
The state of decay
that has eaten away
the state of happiness
that was once my largess

Into the Wild

When I share poems
is there a standing sentry
guarding my intent?
Or do readers have free rein
astride wild galloping minds?

If Only ...

If only I hadn't decided to turn over once more in bed
to rest my eyes for a few more minutes
I woulda, shoulda, coulda
started my day sooner

If only I hadn't dawdled coming down for breakfast,
checking my email and Instagram feed
I woulda, shoulda, coulda
enjoyed my coffee while it was still hot

If only I hadn't debated which sweater to wear
and spent less time trying on different earrings
I woulda, shoulda coulda
been less stressed about getting to my appointment on time

If only I hadn't left my grocery list at home
and remembered which items I needed for dinner
I woulda, shoulda, coulda
eaten something better than the Lean Cuisine in the freezer

If only I hadn't stayed up so late
reading into the wee hours of the morning
I woulda, shoulda, coulda
had a restful night's sleep before the sun came up

Words Align — A Poem Arises

The jumble of random, raucous words,
plucked from dusty volumes,
came together
after shifting, sliding, realigning,
like shards of colored glass in a kaleidoscope,
gaining momentum as ink imprinted paper,
like the jaunty music
flung into the air from a circus calliope
or galloping horses on a carousel,
until the pen came to rest
with a definitive end-stop

Beginnings

In the Beginning . . .
I pause and reflect:
What comes before?
A void or an ending?
A rite of passage?
A thought or an action?
A cause resulting in an effect?

Is the movement from beginning to end
— linear, cyclical, spiraling?
Is it clear where it starts and when?
Is the ending something that happens slowly, silently,
dissipating nearly unnoticed?
Or is it suddenly apparent,
arriving with fanfare, fireworks, headlines
to begin again or anew?

Is the beginning of a life
the moment of conception
or the crowning of a child and its first cry?
Is the beginning of a journey
the planning of an adventure
or the first step on the yellow brick road?
Is the beginning of memory
sounds heard in the womb, moments of clear recall
or photos in an album?

Is the beginning of a poem
a word whispered in a dream, wrapped in a thought,
waiting for my attention?

Selfless Gift

With kindness
her weightless hand
held in mine
I whisper,
"Feel free to leave, if you must
— final rest, no more pain"

Rhythm Of

Knitting needles click in rhythm
when I understand the pattern
of knits and purls
and yarn overs
it flows
— rhythmically, that is

But when the pattern turns complex
and the knits and purls and yarn overs
take on a life of their own
and play hopscotch or leapfrog
or ring-around-the-rosy,
and expect me to chase after them, I lose it;
lose track of what I've just done
— or, lose a stitch

I wonder if that stitch dropped off
mischievously on its own,
just for the sake of doing me in;
the rhythm is broken, it's gone
— and, I'm done in!

Maybe I'll fix it with a quick "tink"
— Knit backwards; get it?
Tink is knit spelled backwards. *Ha!* —
or maybe I'll do a heartrending "frog"
Ribbit! Ribbit! Rip-it! Ha! Ha!
A drastic step that sets me
way back on finishing

Everyone says,
" . . . enjoy the process,"
" . . . it's a journey,"
" . . . take a breath"

But as the rhythm of the seasons flow,
and autumn turns to winter,
will my knitting needles keep up?
Will I have this sweater to keep me warm?

One Day in the Garden of Verses

It all began one quiet afternoon
Humpty Dumpty sat on a wall
While humming to himself
without a care in the world,
a strong gust of wind arose from the west
catching him off guard
and *splat*
— a tragic backward fall
and irreparable damage
that would stymie
all the King's horses and all the King's men
In the adjacent meadow,
under a haystack, fast asleep,
Little Boy Blue
was having a lovely dream that his
sheep's in the meadow
and cow's in the corn
while in fact they had all wandered off
to join the wayward flock belonging to a frantic
Little Bo Peep,
who couldn't tell where to find them!
Just a mere hop, skip and jump away
Little Miss Muffet sat on her tuffet
eating her curds and whey,
lazily gazing as
Jack and Jill went up the hill,
which was lush with green shoots
and masses of bright orange wildflowers
Suddenly came sounds of a commotion
— the clattering of a metal pail,
the splash of spilling water as
Jack fell down and broke his crown
and Jill came tumbling after!
Even though somewhere behind her, a
little dog laughed to see such a sight,
our clear-headed Miss Muffet
sprang into action,
running past the overwhelmed
Old Woman who lived in a shoe
to get medical assistance from

88

Old Mother Hubbard,
who without hesitation,
ignored her whining dog and
went to her cupboard
to fetch iodine and bandages
At the end of the day
all anyone wanted was to have
Polly put the kettle on
— and to have some tea!

I Am a Poem

. . . a gist of an idea
. . . a gush of words
. . . a garden of images
. . . a glint of mischievousness
. . . a glimmer of deep thought
. . . a glow of reflection
. . . a growl of displeasure
. . . a groan of impatience
. . . a grimace of exasperation
. . . a gasp of surprise
. . . a gamble of revelation
. . . a gift of self

Food for Thought

Circling the block, looking for a spot
I happen upon a sign:
"Don't Even Think of Parking Here!"
Why not? Says who?
Always? Sometimes?
What if I want to? What if I dare to?
What would be the harm? What might be the cost?
Risk? Benefit?
Idling in front of the sign; not productive
Waste of gas, waste of time
Waste of brain power
Shift from Park to Drive. Movin' on
Not even gonna think of parking here

Possible Selves

At the self-serious age of seven
I *knew* I would be a teacher
— something I was born to do,
loved to do

I had my hard-cover marble notebooks,
pencils, rulers, paints
I had my cousins join me in "playing school"
I had my life plan

Although I read about student nurses and candy stripers,
secretaries and librarians,
I never saw myself in any of those roles

Although I loved to build with Tinker Toys,
Lincoln Logs, Erector Sets,
create amusement parks and block cities,
I never considered being an architect

Although I loved school plays, painting scenery,
writing stories, learning lyrics and dance steps,
I never thought of a life in theater

I was a child of 1950's TV and mores:
Our Miss Brooks, Captain Kangaroo;
Miss Frances, hostess, of *Ding Dong School*

I lived the plan, became a teacher
of five- and six-year-olds, teachers, administrators,
nieces and nephews and now the "greats"

But now at a self-serious age in my 70s,
Oh, my!
I reflect on present selves,
future selves, possible selves,
and I wonder . . .

The Bedeken

My groom approaches,
trumpet song leads the way:
Od Yishama . . .
So joyful, so sweet

Seated on a throne-like chair,
I await him, watching as he
 — escorted by his father and mine;
 by men singing, dancing, encircling him —
moves towards me

I am surrounded by my mother and his,
by friends and family there to witness, to celebrate
This is the culmination of a week spent apart
With deep love, our eyes meet
 — an intensity, an intimacy, a promise being made

Od yishama b'arei Yehudah
Yet again there shall be heard in the cities of Judah
Uv'chutzot Yerushalayim
And in the streets of Jerusalem
Kol sason v'kol simcha,
The sound of joy and gladness,
Kol chatan, v'kol kallah
The sound of a bridegroom and the sound of a bride

Carefully, he lifts my veil, gently lowering it over my face
The Bedeken: an ancient tradition,
the recognition that I am more than what he sees
 — my inner being is where my true beauty lies

Despite the veil, my vision is clear and strong
He is my heart's desire
At this moment, we become one

Bedeken Haiku

Ancient tradition:
groom veils bride, recognizing
her inner beauty

GLADYS THOMPSON ROTH

Born to Russian immigrants in 1923, Gladys Thompson Roth did not attend kindergarten because her mother thought it "frivolous," instead starting school in first grade. She graduated Samuel J. Tilden High School and Brooklyn College, where she majored in early childhood education, then took postgraduate courses at Queens College en route to earning a Master's Degree in special education from New York University. In the 1940s, she sang "bawdy ballads" in a New Hampshire cocktail lounge, teaching archery and fencing by day to teenaged girls. She later worked for the New York City Board of Education in a variety of roles, from kindergarten teacher to evaluator of children in need of special services — including work as a reading consultant at New York City hospitals. Thompson Roth also served for years as a local director for the feminist organization *Womanspace*. A renowned sculptor working in a range of mediums, among them soapstone, cola-bola wood, onyx, clay, bronze and alabaster, her exhibition *A Journey in Stone and Wood* (2010) was shown in metro-area libraries, universities and galleries — including the Queensborough Community College Art Gallery. Author of two poetry collections, *Sculpted Words* (2016) and *Who I Am* (2022), Thompson Roth was struck in the face by a stray bullet as a child in the Catskills, the gunshot piercing the arm of a boy standing next to her. Eight decades later, the mother of two and grandmother of one even wrote a poem about the experience.

Now is the Winter of My Discontent

(William Shakespeare)
September is here, Summer is over;
the challenge of the sun's warmth
is no longer present
I invite the weather to draw me
into the comfort of the indoors

Tennis and swimming are activities of the past;
listening to music on WQXR and books
on tape provided by the Library of Congress
have become sedentary activities

Family visits enrich my life;
the emerging autumn colors
are dimmed by my failing vision
My 99 years is beginning to show

A Winter Tapestry

I am watching the first snowfall
of the season through my window
It is a week before Spring

The flakes cannot make up their minds;
some are heavy, some are light
They do not stick to the ground;
they stop and start,
they change from left to right
Sometimes, they just come straight down

It is the mercurial wind that is creating
the beautiful display;
does it have something in mind
when the flakes crisscross each other
I feel it is trying to tell me something
Don't quite know what it is;
the artistry eludes me

A redheaded woodpecker, a cardinal
and some sparrows punctuate the scene

Awakening

The warm weather
is deceiving,
the dogwood tree
is holding back

The bare branches
show tight blossoms,
not yet ready
to face the world

Around the bend
the front garden
displays courage;
hyacinths bloom

Daffodils smile,
their yellow gowns
proudly announce
that Spring is here

The Missing Muse

I am trying to write a poem
The thoughts are so mixed,
the ideas so unrelated,
I can't seem to put them together

Where has all the poetry gone,
long time missing
I am worried the ideas are gone forever
I am told it is temporary

The muse will reappear
Don't know where,
don't know when
Long time coming

A Letter in a Bottle

To whom it may concern,
I hope this letter finds you in good health
and high spirits
I have lived one hundred years on this planet
I have done a lot and seen a lot

The Bible tells us that there is an inevitability in the future:
In the last days, nation shall rise up against nation,
kingdom against kingdom
And there shall be famine upon the land and pestilence,
and earthquakes in diverse places

I hope you receive this letter before
all these events become a reality

A Wakeup Call

I woke up this morning
to see the last leaf
fall from my favorite
dogwood tree

I woke up this morning
to see a yellow maple leaf
fall on a mourning dove,
who carried it on its back
until an impatient black squirrel
urged it to fly away

I woke up this morning
to see the first snow
dance with falling leaves

I woke up this morning
to find a whole season gone,
worried about how to keep warm
this long, lonely Winter

I woke up this morning

One Hundred Million Miracles

One hundred million miracles are happening every day:
getting up in the morning, the mechanics of the body;
automatically moving to rise out of bed,
the movement of the fingers
to manage the tools for eating

The changing weather, rapidly from hour-to-hour,
from day to day, is miraculous;
plants growing profusely, changing each day,
miraculous leaves changing their color
provide a beautiful experience

The formation of a relationship, be it a child,
parents or lover; a miracle
I know how babies are born;
still, I think it is a miracle

The healing of a wound,
emotional or physical,
is a miracle

I Am

I am strong
I live in a beautiful house
I used to play tennis
I'd love to take care of myself
I am a word-dancer because I play *Scrabble*
I have two beautiful daughters
I had a handsome husband
I worry about the state of our country
I am helpless
I am hopeful
I am accomplished at human relations
I created a full house of sculptures
I live precariously
I am hanging on

What's in a Lifetime

In a few days I will be
one hundred years old
That is a century!
Much has happened in that time
I grew up, went to school,
graduated, got married,
have two daughters
and one grandson
Earned a Master's Degree
in special education from NYU
Taught for thirty years, until retirement,
then got involved in a women's organization
called *Womanspace*
I also taught a memoir-writing class,
which inspired several women to write their memoirs
Did a lot of traveling, published two books of poetry
— and, one book of my sculptures
When it is said in those few words
it seems like very little
But, it is a whole lifetime

It's hard to focus on what is important
I define my accomplishments
It is for others to define my virtues!

My Last Hurrah

September, Two-Thousand Twenty-Two
I publish my second volume of poetry
It took a lot of courage and encouragement
When it was done I felt depleted of all my feelings
and wondered if I could ever write like this again
The reaction I am getting is inspirational

Not so long ago
I felt strong and successful
The moment was brief

Portrait of a Young Girl

I just created a little girl
She is very shy
Her head tilts to the right
Her arms are folded politely
She is made of wood

Recalcitrant and resistant,
growing up was difficult
Evidence of sharp edges and knots
began to emerge
Taming her was a challenge

With gentle patience,
and careful attention,
her edges were smoothed;
her scars, made invisible

The end result
was sealed, stained
and dressed in new, shiny clothes
She was ready
to face the world

The World is Too Much with Us

The news of the world is otherworldly
The words integrity, honor and compassion,
have lost their meaning
No one is immune. Infants, as well as
old persons are all vulnerable
Is there some solution to the ills of the world?
Wars, tornadoes, buildings collapsing
and fires are more prevalent
and devastating than ever
Although, miracles *do* happen: four children,
ages thirteen, nine, four and one
— found alive forty days after a Colombian plane crash
If this poem makes no sense, it is because
I have not been able to make sense
of the world

April in Paris

We spent nine Aprils in Paris
Marty chartered a plane to take young internationals,
who lived in the YMCA on West 53rd Street in Manhattan
They were going to visit their families in Europe

My first time in Paris, Marty and I
stayed at the Hotel Regina;
luxuriated in our room, which was like a French boudoir,
with red upholstery, brass bed post
and doorknobs
The elevator was an open cage

Ate at Tour d'Argent
and tasted wine in the wine cellar
Sat in open air cafes, remembered
Sartre, Stein, Hemmingway and Picasso
Saw the da Vinci Mona Lisa
and Monet water lilies
Saw Chartres and Notre Dame
Walked along the Seine,
enjoyed seeing young people
openly embracing

One April it was quite chilly;
bought myself a woolen suit
in a chic boutique
This was the beginning
of my addiction to travel

A Good Deed

When we bought
the house on Briar Lane
we were sure it would be
good for my parents to share;
no staircase to climb
My dad died;
could not enjoy it
My mother shared our house
'til she was one hundred and four
Now, I enjoy it

I Forgot to Mention

Oops, I forgot to mention
in my list of accomplishments
my experience singing in a hotel
cocktail lounge
It was the Hotel Sinclair
in Bethlehem, New Hampshire
I got the job through
an advertisement in
The New York Times
In the interview I played the piano
to accompany myself, saying:
My guitar is being repaired
My repertoire consisted of bawdy ballads,
which are really sea shanties
The hotel had a dance band
The boys in the band were very helpful
in grooming me with the appropriate
chords on my guitar
I had just met Marty
and he flew up to see me perform
He brought a guest from the hotel
to the cocktail lounge
They had a drink together
After they were finished he threw
a tip over his shoulder and said:
I want it back later

A Vague Memory

The summer of Nineteen-Thirty-Five
I, twelve years old, sat on a fence
watching bugs crawl by
Suddenly, a shot was heard;
a bullet hit my chin
I put my hand up to stem the flow of blood;
it felt like my chin was gone
The same bullet hit a seven-year-old
standing next to me; went through
the fleshy part of his upper arm

100

We were sent for tetanus shots,
then sent home; end of story
No follow up, no reprimand;
no investigation, no further discussion
Difficult to remember,
no one left to verify
No evidence of the incident
— except for the scar
under my chin

Lest We Forget

It was Memorial Day
I was looking for something in my closet
I opened many garment bags
Suddenly, I saw my husband's
First Lieutenant's uniform
I had never seen him in it
When we met, he was already
out of uniform
A chill went through me
when I imagined what this uniform experienced;
the hair-raising escapes in his airplane,
the brush with death on so many occasions
The uniform came alive
I can see his handsome body
— and, yearn for it

Because

Because it's so lonely without you
Because your presence is felt by your absence
Because so much of me is you
Because every joy in my life I shared with you
Because you were always by my side
Because *problems were only opportunities in disguise*
Because our daughters reflect your wit
Because I am bereft
Because the world is changed
Because time is not a great healer
Because I need to write about you

101

GEORGE PAFITIS

Born in Astoria, New York, in 1939, George Pafitis grew up playing stickball and handball when he couldn't find a a baseball game. A graduate of William Cullen Bryant High School, he attended night school at Brooklyn College, then graduated New York Community College before earning a degree in chemistry at Long Island University. Working as a chemist, Pafitis earned an MBA in Marketing and sold air time for radio stations throughout the 1970s, later selling air time for TV before being forced into retirement in 2002 as he battled non-Hodgkin's lymphoma. During that time, Pafitis joined a poetry workshop at the Great Neck Community Education Center in Nassau County, Long Island, beginning a love affair with poetry that he's described as "a joyful, pleasurable and rewarding pursuit." He attends and participates in Performance Poets Associates (PPA) readings and other Long Island poetry events and his poems have been published in the PPA, Literary Review and NCPLS (Nassau County Poet Laureate Society) Review. He has published two books — *Feelings and Words Traveling Together* in 2014; and, *Feelings and Words Traveling Together Volume 2* in 2016. Pafitis also hosts a monthly reading series at the Great Neck Public Library, where featured readers present their poems, followed by an open mic.

The Sound of Onomatopoeia

The chug of garbage truck wakes me,
gives me a buzz between my ears,
causing my brain to slosh around in my head

But I murmur to myself, go on with my day
I pop my daily pills into my mouth
— and, with a splash of water, gulp them down

I swish up my face with a splash of water in the shower
and patter my body with soapy suds

I mop my body up and as I look out the window
I see a whisper of light fall from the sky

After which a trickle of water comes down;
then, a clash of thunder from the clouds
crashing into each other

Finally, rain pours down
like colorless soap bubbles,
splish-splashing all over,
before trickling into drains

A Ritual

The first glass of wine
swallowed so fine

It held them together
until the day broke

Then, the glass from which they drank
put them asleep, as if on top of a plank

But, once awake they felt like
wading in a *backveld*

Feeling overwhelmed, thus they waited
— 'til the beds of the seas dehydrated

And, after the tide went out
they then awoke to scout

The Corked Bottle

The corked bottle with a message enclosed;
floating in the sea, asking for *Help!*

A decision must be made in a dispute
If I concede to the extreme it would offer a heavy
strain on me, and only me. If I stand firm, dug in, concrete,
it would be equally as contentious

Is there a conciliatory path leaning several ways
from the middle to the end I could choose?

I'll ruminate, illuminate, nominate,
until I find — or, not find — the corked bottle

It is not likely I will find the corked bottle;
the sea is big, busy — and deep . . .

And, the message enclosed will say:
Stand tall, lock your heels,
be self-reliant and thus decide
I know. I wrote it

Entrances and Exits

He pushed her,
strangled her thoughts of fairness
Why did he want
more than fair?

Wounded, angry,
never felt good about himself;
lacked enough
self-recognition

Probably felt under-appreciated
in nuclear family, not clear-headed,
thoughts cloudy
about contacts and events

In essence
was trapped in his own prison,
bursting out
at an older sibling

Smothered mother's sense
of justice,
depriving himself
of comity in living

Life is unfair at times
But, be assured,
life is worthy

Color in Our Lives

The leaves of Autumn are multicolored,
making us sense change approaches
Color comes through, sight affecting us

Fashion designers select hues to flatter our self image;
their selections prompt us to view ourselves colorfully
Our feelings and thoughts are influenced by color

Sunrise and dusk offer striking impressions of coloration,
impacting on our sense of nature's beauty
Color comes through, sight affecting us

The Fourth of July fireworks offer us the joy of patriotism
 — and, the potential of war
Through the vision of fire and explosions
our feelings and thoughts are influenced by color

The stark blue skies, along with bright sun, is joyous;
when the sky dims to a flat gray our inner vision recalls
Color comes through, sight affecting us

Though the radiance of the light spectrum is upon us,
on and off, we will nourish coloring as edifying
Color comes through, sight affecting us
Our feelings and thoughts are influenced by color

Four Stanzas, Four Lines, Four Syllables

The tree trunk, big,
bulbous, like leg
of prehistoric
elephant long-gone

Sits tight, firm to
the ground, where roots
reach deep in Earth,
bracing the tree

Firm into Earth,
then reaching up,
straight to the clouds
— where heaven shows

And, at trunk base
squirrels dig-up
dirt, unearthing
nuts for nutrition

The Lonely Coffee Cup

Three people go to a coffee shop late at night
It is spacious, well-lighted
— yet, somehow, inspires lonesomeness
A man sits with his back toward us,
as we look in through the large
plate-glass window
The couple at the other end of counter
sits looking out at what seems like
peering into nothingness, smoking
All three people are oblivious
to each other; wearing bewitching expressions,
not recognizing even themselves
They have one thing in common:
their supreme loneliness in the big city
with millions of people

The diner itself implies space; it is roomy,
big and captures distance
— which implies loneliness
And those thick white mugs
are the epitome of drowning themselves
with a narcotic

Character Matters

Thought is common to all of us
and leads to feelings, which is
the purview of human character

Character matters

When certain of these thoughts
reach out and create antagonistic
feelings offering anger, rage, acrimony,
on any level, it should be accepted as
human frailty — and, be tolerated evenly

Character matters

But, it should not smother the common
humanity, beginning with shared speech,
common ground, simple decency, kindness

Character matters

And, more important, the deep humanity
of sharing, participating in the human
experience of justice, peace, joy
— all, through the umbrella
of genuine human love

Character matters

Which takes us to the provenance
of humankind, our ultimate purpose

Character must matter

Let Us Go

Let us go then you and I,
to wonder about thoughts
and feelings, to offer
an understanding of so
much encircling us

Trees, bare of leaves,
infectious diseases abound;
excess heat, flooding;
political turmoil;
economic depravation

Let us go and prepare
thoughts to face these challenges;
we should face and meet faces
to help us explore solutions
I know not what more to say or believe

Indecision is a scourge;
the days are not the same,
running into each other without purpose
Strive, seek and not surrender,
seize the day

Let us go then, you and I

Where to Be

Sparsely populated mountainous
states like Montana, Wyoming,
where Amtrak trains roar
through the edges of mountains
We most wonder what occurs
to the bears, wolves, pumas,
as they look at these long
stretches of steel

Thundering along these tracks
at such high speeds

108

Does the wolf salivate when
seeing human heads pass along
Does the bear clamor about
the succulent human flesh it sees
And the puma? Does it activate
its jaw muscles for a bite

We know the power of the senses
of these beautiful beasts
But we must ponder:
What are *they* thinking?

An I Am Poem

I am: Multidimensional, but I get confused
by some of the dimensions; they are cryptic
I live in: A comfortable place when I cancel out
the discomforts of all sorts; which is difficult to do
I used to: Write poorly; now, I just write
— and, consider what I write critically!

I'd love: To be more into thinking and feeling
about my writings with outside commentary
I am a word-dancer: Yes, indeed I enjoy words
as they dance around my head
I have: Memories of breathing more freely
than I do now (since the lung surgery)

I had: Concerns about running out of my inhaler;
which is unwarranted
I worry about: Running out of rubber bands
— and staples!
I am: Happy and confused by some of my writings

I am accomplished: I feel my writings
and continue to wonder about them!

I live: In a happy place most of the time;
especially, when the heat
and electricity is working properly

Poetry is Motion and Sound

Poetry is motion, full;
the words move vigorously
along the line, by rhythm or rhyme

Poetry offers firmly wrapped
lines that sizzle as they move
along the page

The impact of the sparkle of words
as they move, prompts feelings
that circulate around the brain,
lighting up sense impressions
with sounds that echo
off the walls of the mind,
setting up melodic energy;
matching motion with sound,
offering multidimensional grasps
of feelings

The Ride to Nowhere but Beauty

As we drive along the streets to a someplace
we face signs directing us to do
— or not to do:

Stop. Go Slow. Parking Ahead
Red Light Signal. Sign with Arrows. Yield Right
Caution School Ahead. No Horn Blowing
All necessary, needed for safety and civility
But, no mention, nothing about the beauty
of the drive amidst the wealth
of trees, grass, bushes;
all the vegetation, with its myriad
colors of green, aided by so many hues;
shades, with textures of green
that enliven our eyes,
and leave us to marvel at something as natural
as the Spring vegetation
of glorious green

A Portrait for Finding Light

Table set, fork missing,
glass forgotten,
steps taken, all's well
At last, time for repast

Chairs placed,
eyes latch to eyes;
the smell of fresh bread, cheese,
drips with scent of good taste

The satisfied palate
enlivens conversation,
a momentary
diversion

But eyes look deeper,
magnetic fields ignite an attraction,
meshing into a shared recollection
of distress

Child told to leave,
house torn apart;
shared pleasures lost,
unity ripped asunder

The flame of discord
always flickered;
in time, grew into a deluge
— leaving ashes

Time is now,
what is done is done;
go on to what should be done,
chase the light

Seek visual stimulation,
leave darkness behind;
uncover accommodation,
meet fulfillment

The somberness of dusk
always leads to brightness of daylight

VICTORIA BJORKLUND

Victoria B. Bjorklund is a retired partner at the international law firm Simpson Thacher & Bartlett LLP, where she founded and for 30 years headed the Firm's Exempt Organizations Group advising nonprofits, their boards, and donors. She taught The Law of Nonprofits at Harvard Law School and is co-author of the treatise *New York Nonprofit Law and Practice* — the treatise most-cited by New York State Courts. In 1989, Victoria helped found Doctors Without Borders USA as its first U.S. volunteer and continues as Chair of its Board of Advisors. She is a long-time director of the Robin Hood Foundation, leading the COVID-19, Superstorm Sandy and 9/11 Relief Funds, and serves on the boards of The Institute for Advanced Study, Lawyers Committee for Civil Rights Under Law, Friends of Fondation de France — and, until recently, The Louvre Endowment in Paris, American Friends of the Louvre, Princeton University and Nutrition Science Initiative. She also volunteers with the Concussion Legacy Foundation. Victoria was in the first class of women at Princeton, graduated in three years, was Princeton's first women's basketball player and was among the first women elected to Phi Beta Kappa. She earned her Ph.D. in Medieval Studies from Yale and J.D. from Columbia School of Law. A specialist in manuscripts of the little-studied Anglo-Norman dialect spoken by Viking invaders in Norman France, Victoria learned through DNA and genealogical research she is, in fact, a descendent of Vikings who spoke Anglo-Norman.

Seaside Attractions

On the bench
by the sea
my demented mother and I
sat for hours

I chirped with chit chat,
but the discussion,
being one-sided,
faded out

So we listened
to the buoy bell
clanging hypnotically
in rhythm with the soft waves

What attracts us to the sea,
this way, I murmured
Because we all came out of
the water, she replied

Apostrophe & Comma, The Punctuation Twins

Oh
little mark
hangin' in the air,
so much lighter
than its lyin' low
twin,
who signals
take a breath,
take a break,
all the while it floats
above the line like a
magic wand of
possession or omission;
so powerful
by its *itsy bitsy* little self
— it's how its story gets told

113

The Narwhal Tusk

(London Attacker Subdued by Man Wielding Narwhal Tusk)
*"There's something very British about fighting a terrorist with a
narwhal tusk," said historian Guy Walters. "We don't carry
weapons in this country. But we do have narwhal tusks around."*

Behold the narwhal's ivory tooth:
Its helix spiral born in the Arctic deep,
its name from the Old Norse
for corpse whale, so pale and mottled is it,
like the skin of a dead man left too long in frigid waters

But no man grows a tooth like the corpse whale
This tusk became an object of desire ages ago
This, clever Vikings saw, could bring them great riches
from flatlander kings; Ivan the Terrible had one at his death bed,
Elizabeth I had several, and Phillip II possessed a dozen more

To protect from poisoning,
as symbol of the Christ-like unicorn,
as novelty of the Renaissance wonder room,
from decoration of the Fishmonger's Hall,
become lance outside its dusty walls

So the narwhal's ancient tusk
again protected men,
again was wielded, not against
another in the dark or poison in the dinner,
but against an angry man on a bridge

Tidal Force Tanka

Hail the blood-red moon
floating high up in the sky,
guardian of tides
— extra low and extra high;
nightlight for my love and I

Who watch its shadows
float at our chamber ceiling,
urging eyes to close

When we wake in the morning
we will see a sinking bulb

That will grow and wane
on future nights, its beauty
to unfold upon
sea creatures doing tidal
things in tidal pools below

My love and I think
tidal thoughts as we lie in
our dark bed, contemplating
that tidal moon exerting
its tidal force on us all

My Seventh Generation

"...the sunrise of forever
Just ahead of us, through the trees
One generation after the other." — Joy Harjo

Six generations ago
my Protestant forefather escaped Catholic hatred by
fleeing in dead of night from Palatine Germany
to Palatine, New York

Six generations ago
my foremother escaped white-settler hatred by
assimilating, being adopted from her Mohawk tribe
into a family of white persons

Three generations ago
a disdainful genealogist
tut-tutted that, as an "older man" of thirty-six,
great-great-great grandfather
"married outside his race"

In the 21st century
my seventh-generation DNA
tells me I am a product of the mating
of Old Ackerman and the native woman,
from one of their eight children, who lived and loved,
one generation after the other

115

The Red Nun and Her Lover

Hear the red nun
clanking in the dark,
her buoy bell in chamber
rocking to and fro,
tethered to the sand
by umbilical cord
of iron links

What was left of Horace
was scattered at her base,
his dust drifting downward to
the silt, the sand,
so that he could forever
be with her, his love;
to hear her song of warning:
Stay right! Stay right!
Red, right, returning;
morning, noon, and night

Sally has the Last Laugh

Enslaved maidservant
and sister-in-law to Thomas Jefferson,
Sally Hemings,
was good enough
to bear him six children
But,
the master hypocrite
was not good enough
to acknowledge them
as his children
— until his
pesky Y-chromosome
did the talking
for him

116

Your First and Last Acts

I am the first and will be the last act of your life
I am with you 25,000 times a day
But, how often do you think of me
— except, when you need me?

I was manipulated by the iron cylinders
that terrified children of the 1950s
and, now, by the thumped hissing of COVID fear
that you politely call a respirator

I can be timed or trained
But, my truth is that you can neither
have too much of me
— nor hold me too long

Breath is the metaphor of the universe:
Take in what you need,
pour back when you are done
I am the first and will be the last act of your life

Zoom Attacks

I try to work on Zoom all day
But, you arrive and want to stay
Right on my keyboard in the way
And, block what points I have to say

You're the cutest cat I ever saw
That's why there ought to be a law
That you can't distract me with your paw
Or purr or lick to stroke your jaw

To work from home, it's just a fact
That you're here, too, and will distract
Me from the work on online causes
That's just why we need those *lawses!*

Floating to the Moon (Partial Cento)

The wind was a torrent of darkness among the gusty trees;
the moon was a ghostly galleon tossed upon cloudy seas
The moon, like a flower in heaven's high bower,
with silent delight sits and smiles on the night

They danced by the light of the moon, the moon,
the moon, they danced by the light of the moon
Slowly, silently, now the moon
walks the night in her silver *schoon*

And I float below in the Atlantic sea,
wondering if I let the current pull me
away from the shore would I float to Cancun
or float up the white ribbon — all the way to the moon?

The Kitchen Table

I was once the littlest one
brought to
great-grandmother's kaffeeklatsch
by my glamorous mother;
her well-cut tweed suit,
her lacquered red nails,
her matching lipstick,
her crocodile pumps

They passed around little me
for hugs and kisses,
oohs and *aahs,*
so many of my mother's
female relatives
all chattering with their news

One of my earliest memories:
their legs, their stockings, their practical black shoes,
my mother's fashionable crocodile pumps

Four generations of women
— my great-grandmother,
my great-aunts,
my grandmother,
my mother,
little me
They, sitting around;
me, sitting under
the enamel-top kitchen table,
staying close by the crocodile pumps

Orange Emergency

Shall I order a bouquet for
your centerpiece?
She hesitated (evaluating my competence)
Well, that *would* help with the event

I telephoned her elderly florist
(such a kind man)
I want a spectacular centerpiece,
huge sprays of gorgeous flowers

What colors? he asked
Anything but orange, I replied,
knowing she detested orange;
knowing her artist's pastel palette

The day arrived, as did the centerpiece
It was lavish, it was huge. It was *orange*
Nothing *but* orange
I gasped, agape

The florist was flummoxed
Notes were checked
Oh, "Anything, *but* orange"
Not "anything orange"

No worries;
someone else will love it
We always keep a spare
For emergencies, we keep pastels

Levitation

Magritte's floating rocks,
suspended mid-sky,
above the ocean,
above the castle,
above the clouds,
Oh, that I might
levitate like
those rocks,
permanently oblivious to
yank of gravity
Or, that I might
lie safely below,
in their shadows,
trusting them
floating just above
If only we could levitate
our worries
like those rocks levitate,
having their assurance they will not
change their minds
— and crush us

Cloaking My Vocabulary

When my computer instructs me
to provide new passwords
I strive mightily at the anvil of my vocabulary,
I swim the sea of indecipherable words,
I sail to Ultima Thule 33
— where the wind is too harsh for hackers
I urge the waters of *Seljalandsfoss*
to gush verbosely from the spigot
of ancient dictionaries
Snorri Sturluson can choose my choices,
making Freya, Thor, and Loki,
my companions in
might, strength and trickery;
my password vocabulary wears
the cloak of invincibility

120

How to Fall Asleep

When I struggle to fall asleep
I count *"shun"* words instead of sheep:
Admiration, Benediction
Celebration, Dedication
Elaboration, Felicitation
Graduation, Habitation
Iteration, Justification
Kleptomation, Libation
Mastication, Notification
Operation, Pontification
Quadruplication, Reformation
Salutation, Titration
Undulation, Vacation
Weatherization, X-radiation
But, then I come to Y and Z,
by which time I better be
asleep as my *"shun"* words
have abandoned me!

The Worst Food My Parents Made Me Eat

It wasn't liver,
though obviously that
was so bad it had to be
smothered in fried onions
It wasn't haggis,
though that was cooked only
during visits of the Scottish cousin
before importation of sheep offal was banned
It wasn't lutefisk,
though that Scandinavian delicacy
of codfish soaked in lye until gelatinous
smelled a lot like sweaty feet
No, it was pancakes!
Those white-flour pads pasted,
Elmer's-gluelike,
to the roof of my mouth,
adhered there by too-too-sweet syrup
To this day I avert my eyes
at the stomach-churning sight of IHOP

121

EVELYN KANDEL

Evelyn Kandel served as Nassau County Poet Laureate from 2019-2022. While the pandemic made it difficult for in-person readings and library time with children, she continued her adult poetry class using Zoom. Author of six books of poetry, her most recent, *Let There Be Clouds,* includes her photographs of the sky — taken daily for a month, each accompanied by a poem. Her work has appeared in journals and anthologies, most recently in *COVID*, edited by Gayl Teller, and *Paumanok Transition*, edited by Kathaleen Donnelly. During the Korean War Kandel became one of the earliest women to enlist in the U.S. Marine Corps, attaining the rank of Sergeant. In 1952, she was one of four women — Army, Air Force, Navy, Marines — to represent the military on a U.S. Postage Stamp titled *Women in Our Armed Services*. She also was featured on recruiting posters. "They said, 'Hey, gorgeous. We Want You!'" Kandel recalled. Post-military, Kandel studied at Columbia University on the GI Bill, then worked as an art teacher and department head at exclusive Portledge School, retiring in 1999. She turned from painting to small sculptures and poetry during a residency in Saratoga, then began focusing on poetry alone. Since 2009 she has taught Writing Poetry and has since inspired countless poets. This is her fourth class anthology.

My Fantasy Garden

Everyone is planting their gardens
with flowers of all types and size
Everyone is choosing the colors
that will look best
There is a rush to go to the garden centers
— to be the first to find
the newest variety of an old favorite,
one that will blossom from Spring to Fall
and return next year
Ooh lovely, to be the first,
to display this novelty
To proudly accept all compliments
Everyone is digging and feeding
and planting everything they bought
Well, *wait!*
Everyone but one — that's me
I have planted a Fantasy Garden,
a work of creativity like none other
I have not planted or weeded
or watered for my art exhibit
I have not bought seeds
or special food for the garden
No, it is not needed
or need to be weeded
because my garden is . . .
A work of art from a not-natural source,
but bought from a store
It is from a fake-flower department
with all-color blossoms galore
So, I cut the wire stems short
and cut the bouquets into parts,
then placed them in the ground
in a profusion of yellows and blues,
purple and orange
 and green leaves between
Then made a beautiful sign
showing flowers and the words:
FANTASY GARDEN
— and it's so fine!!

Yesterday the Day Broke

Not like dawn breaking
over a mountain lake,
more a raging flood
overwhelming
a sleeping town

More a heart breaking,
blood surging from arteries,
beads of blood on palms
— beyond stigmata

Yesterday, words burst
from throats raw with emotion,
no longer contained
Tears spurting in hot release
from rusted steam pipes
in a cellar of unmet needs

At night
thoughts of yesterday's
wounding break,
so frightening
they will not be soothed
— destroying my sleep

Winter Sounds

Wrapped in its gray cloak,
the sky is crying
Tear drops on the window,
ask to be let in to dry
Backyard pine trees are praying
The rise and fall of their whispers
are quiet as they bend
in somber supplication
Even the wailing wind is mournful,
barely lifting small delicate branches
waving at the top of massive oaks

Oh, enough with the howling winds,
the threat of snow turning to sleet
Instead,
could we not hear the rustle
of Spring leaves?
Or listen to a choir of birds,
loudly singing,
from the phone lines?

What About Trees?

How many poems have been
written about trees?
A thousand?
A hundred-thousand?

But not these trees
These are New York trees
These are Nassau County
on Long Island trees,
on Nassau County roads
out to Suffolk County

These are trees that are assertive,
that reach out across the road
Greet one another over your head
as you drive under them
And, I love that

When driving for an appointment
that, somehow, I'm late for,
it doesn't seem to bother me,
because trees are so entertaining

They rustle, they shake in the breeze
They reach across your head
As you drive under them, they drop
lots of stuff to make you sneeze
They do things to frighten you,
sometimes do things to please
No matter what they do,
I love trees

125

There are Good Times

There are good times,
there are bad times,
some so sad you cannot
continue to live with them
and turn away from
the good folks
who call and sympathize
and empathize,
pat your back
and hold your hand

You turn away,
you run away

Or you pretend that all
is fine and you are doing well;
you join the fun and turn
from one thing to another,
until one day

You run away again

Outside the window,
trees are shaking their
new green leaves
and sun glints against glass,
turning it into
golden diamonds
that dazzle your eyes, make

You turn away again

Going inside where the room
is dim and silent,
music brings tears to bathe
memories and drown pain
There is a sweetness
to yesterday that calms

You no longer turn away

Where Do Poems Come From?

"Poetry seems especially like nothing else.
It is the very lining of the inner life." — C.D. Wright

Where do my poems live before I write them?
In the slit between a door standing ajar
and the outside steps

I slip through, hide in a dark corner
until courage returns, to begin
a tentative journey
My imagination dons wings;
floor, walls, disappear
I rise, I fly above wondering
thoughts, unresolved troubles,
find new pathways,
avoid circular mazes

Sometimes, it leads to blank pages
Other times, my pen scratches the soft,
white surface, words stored in my mind appear;
the poem, born in a doorway,
writes itself in the sweet outdoors

The Last Touch

When I walk in the world
through the city streets
without your steps beside me
I pass loneliness lurking behind
a door into our dark house
If I open that door
I find only still, empty rooms
where once there was your laughter
filling my ears and heart
Now, I live with shifting memories
and cannot bring your face into focus;
sounds of comfort blur and fade
— and gone,
the last touch of your hand

127

IN REMEMBRANCE

Poems from Two
Beloved Class Members
Who've Left Us

Jack B. Weinstein

Old Slights

My physical life slowly ending,
each night new incriminations
flood my mind of slights to others I loved:
sons, pulling at my sleeve to play catch,
pushed off, so I could write
books — sitting on shelves;
rebuff to spouse I doted on,
who asked to see movie,
meet friends for merry dinners;
missed opportunities to kiss warm,
naked neck when she turned to me
in love as we dressed;
silence in unspoken thoughts on day's
work and events that might have drawn us closer
Now, separated by death's gate,
there is no way to apologize
A new love permits
lesson learned to be applied:
Express affection when you can

Do We Need to Kill?

Atomic bombs dropped. We spot a merchant ship
Captain orders approach: "Ready One!"
Next to him, at radar screen, I whisper:
"War is almost over, probably civilians aboard
Do we need to kill?"
"We have our orders: 'Sink, until surrender'"
"Range?"
"Two-thousand yards"
"Fire One!"
Maru explodes, sinks. No survivors
August 1945. I join crew's cheer
Do not forget: I killed

Born in Wichita, Kansas, 1921, Weinstein attended Lincoln High School, Brooklyn College
and Columbia University Law, serving on the sub *U.S.S. Jallao* in World War II. A notable
U.S. District Court Judge for the Eastern District of New York, he died at 99 in 2021.

AARON REISFELD

Peregrinations

Autumn morning dawned in resplendent hues of gold,
painted on azure sky by sun, rising on horizon,
bathing my bedroom in soft light
It roused me from slumber, laced with youthful dreams
in surge of newly awake hormones

This would be the last, in long time, to sleep peacefully
in my own bed, as boom of window-shattering
explosions proclaimed start of war, terminating
my boyhood — and dragging me into seething cauldron
of warfare and wanderings over four continents

The fire-breathing Nazi dragon poised like coiled cobra,
ready to start devouring Europe in bloody Apocalypse,
its bombers, like vultures, spreading terror, death on innocents,
including myself, just turned seventeen

Soldiers came to our house, conscripting me
into the Polish Army, as mother shrieked:
"Let him go, he is only a boy!"
Parting from her, she yelped in despair:
"I'll never see you again!"
Alas, she would never, as the winds of war
blew me all over the tortured lands
of Europe, Africa and Asia

Sometimes, when winds howl between the trees,
I think I can hear my mother's prophetic plaint:
"I'll never see you again!"
— bringing back that moment of our parting
and my life-long trauma

Why did it all have to happen?
That question trembles on my lips
But, who is there to answer?

Born in Lodz, Poland, 1922, Reisfeld served in the Polish, British and Israeli armies, graduated Nottingham College, emigrated to the U.S. in 1949, founded a consulting firm and authored *To Run for Life from Swastika and Red Star*. He died at 100 in 2022.

APPENDIX

Gladys Thompson Roth
Now is the Winter of My Discontent. A Winter Tapestry. Awakening. The Missing Muse. A Letter in a Bottle. A Wakeup Call. One Hundred Million Miracles. I Am. What's in a Lifetime. My Last Hurrah. Portrait of a Young Girl. The World is Too Much with Us. April in Paris. A Good Deed. I Forgot to Mention. A Vague Memory. Lest We Forget. Because. Used with permission. Copyright © 2017, 2022, 2023 by Gladys Thompson Roth.

Sheila Saferstein
Shade. Medea. Ode to Antiquity. Of Me I Sing. Moonlit Memories. Life Lessons. Season's Changes. Your Gifts. Curiosities. Cleanse. Gone. Closets are Not to Store Tangibles. My Poem May Be a Hit of Mythic Proportions. My Metaphorical Musings on Seasons. Land of Enchantment. Used with permission. Copyright © 2022, 2023 by Sheila Saferstein.

George Strausman
Wondering. What If? Words. Woman. The Real Genie. Miracles. My Little Girl. Picnic Ready. Aging. Plurals. Someday (2014, 2022). Time. No Regrets. Your Love. Signs of Youth. I Yam. I Wonder. Used with permission. Copyright © 2014, 2022, 2023 by George Strausman.

John A. Valenti 3rd
It's Us, Not Them. Penn Station, 1985. A Bottle Thrown. Grandma's Kitchen, Mine. Some Men. Get the Picture. My Old Man. Metal Fatigue. On the Platform. I'm Tired. Change Come Slow. The Train Car. Used with permission. Copyright © 1983, 1985, 2022, 2023 by John A. Valenti 3rd.

Susan Aster Wallman
Marilyn's Mattress. Me and Pooh. Go Figure! Alive, but . . . Shadorma Forma, Three Times I Conforma. Wait . . . They Will Come. A Legs Rap. Ode to Nothingness. State of Grace. Birth of a Notion. Uncanny Happening. Pintimacy. Reverie at Dawn. Used with permission. Copyright © 2022, 2023 by Susan Aster Wallman.

Jack B. Weinstein
Old Slights. Do We Need to Kill? Used with permission. Copyright © 2016 by Jack B. Weinstein.

Judith Zilberstein
Armed and Dangerous. The Age of Ists. An Itty Bitty Ditty. Rat-a-Tat-Tat. Metaphorically Speaking. Himself. A Whale Tale. A Series of Unfortunate Events. Weather Head. Portrait. Good Indeed. Through the Pain. At the End of the Day. Bitter Herbs. Used with permission. Copyright © 2022, 2023 by Judith Zilberstein.